THE EVIL AT MONTEINE

Richard Ulrome worked for billionaire recluse Simon Miaolo. At first, Anne Blackwell was pleased for her fiancé's career. But then it seemed that Richard was a prisoner at Monteine Castle, Miaolo's headquarters. Anne realized that a master of Evil in a satanic ritual of sacrifice and renewal was manipulating Richard and herself. And like others before her, Anne turned to Ruane the Witchfinder. A man who would listen. A man waging a private war against the Devil.

Books by Brian Ball
in the Linford Mystery Library:

DEATH OF A LOW HANDICAP MAN
MONTENEGRIN GOLD
THE VENOMOUS SERPENT
MALICE OF THE SOUL
DEATH ON THE DRIVING RANGE
DEVIL'S PEAK
MARK OF THE BEAST

BRIAN BALL

THE EVIL AT MONTEINE

Complete and Unabridged

LINFORD
Leicester

First published in Great Britain

First Linford Edition
published 2010

British Library CIP Data

Ball, Brian, *1932* –
The evil at Monteine. - -
(Linford mystery library)
1. Satanism– –Fiction. 2. Occult fiction.
3. Large type books.
I. Title II. Series
823.9′14–dc22

ISBN 978–1–44480–104–0

Published by
F. A. Thorpe (Publishing)
Anstey, Leicestershire

Set by Words & Graphics Ltd.
Anstey, Leicestershire
Printed and bound in Great Britain by
T. J. International Ltd., Padstow, Cornwall

This book is printed on acid-free paper

1

I had decided to drive on to Monteine. I wanted to speak to Richard Ulrome at Monteine Castle, International Marine Oils Promotion, Research and Projects Division.

'You're demeaning yourself, girl,' I told myself. 'You're chasing him. If he can't take the trouble to ring every day, the hell with him.'

The visit was to have been a pleasant surprise for him. It showed I cared about the sponsorship he was after. I had worked out what I'd tell him.

I'd be calm and polite when I told Richard I'd arrived to talk about us, and what the hell was I supposed to do when he sailed away for the Three-Oceans Race. 'You think I'm going to sit at home waiting?' I intended to say. 'Not me. You can't ask me to stay home knitting sweaters for twelve whole months, can you? Then I'd tell him he wasn't the only man around and what did he think of that? I was going to tell him that I couldn't wait around for a winter and a spring and a summer and an autumn. Who can? Not me', I told myself. Not Anne Blackwell.

I was as mixed up as it's possible to be by the time I saw the North Sea. On the North Yorkshire Coast you have to drive along the tops of six-hundred-foot cliffs, and the sea fills your horizon, stretching out with a grey insistence to the Arctic. Thick cloud covered the sky. The coast, the cliffs and the sea weren't the cheeriest of sights, nor was Monteine Castle.

It reared up on a colossal shelf of grey stone on the highest promontory for miles. The Castle had been built around and into this grey pinnacle. Two enormous turrets surmounted a massive keep, built on three levels, each with its crenellated and castellated curtain walls. There was no sign of ruin or decay: the Castle was intact, a forbidding mass that dominated the sweep of Monteine Bay and the small fishing town six hundred feet below.

Monteine Castle was ugly and menacing, in the way that some old buildings can be. By the time I drove up the newly asphalted road that led to the lodge gates, I felt like turning back to the little town in the bay.

Not two miles from the Castle was Monteine Landing, the little town that got some sort of a living from a couple of pubs with summer accommodation and what's left of the inshore fish. I'd seen fishing-cobbles, and red-faced men shaking with laughter as they finished their beer when I'd driven up the long, winding road to the Castle.

If I couldn't get a bed at Monteine Landing, I'd have tea and drive back to finish my Harrogate assignment, then ring through to my son's Aunt Gloria to have her tell him that Mummy would be back that night. I didn't want to face Richard.

Would you believe it, he spotted my Fiat as I turned.

'Anne!' he mouthed. I didn't hear him for I over-revved the engine the way I'd been told not to by a succession of men

3

from Tony's father onwards. 'Anne!'

I saw him waving in the mirror. Richard has a tanned, clear skin. There's no sign of a wrinkle though he's in his mid-thirties. His frame has the deceptive slimness of an athlete. I thought he was undernourished when I first met him, which was at one of Freda Langdon's parties just after he'd raced in what yachtsmen call the South Atlantic Triangle. He came second because he'd been blown off-course by a fierce January storm. He wasn't exactly a household word, but he was one of the top dozen of his kind.

I remember staring at him and deciding in the same instant I wanted him. A nice Scottish electronics engineer I'd been with for a month or two without any real commitment on my part saw the look I gave Richard; he said something to me about leaving, but he must have suspected at once that our affair was over.

A week after the party the Scot conceded defeat and Richard and I had a marvellous five months. I knew I was in love with him when he said he'd entered

4

another race, one that would take him away for the best part of a year. I tried very hard not to show my sheer dismay, then in the morning it hit me that I wouldn't see him for weeks, then months, then a whole year,

The trouble was that I'd got used to being hurt till Richard, then I didn't want the kicks any more. I came from a miserable home. My parents were grocers who sold out a prime site to a supermarket chain and went to live in Majorca when I was sixteen. They didn't like me, never had; they didn't like one another much either. My father was fifty-one when he married my mother, who herself was in her late thirties. She'd been his shop assistant. I think of them in that grocer's shop knowing one another too well and getting married for no other reason than that I was on the way. They didn't want me in Majorca because I was into mild drugs at fourteen and experimenting with acid at sixteen, which was when I dropped out of school, home and everything else I'd known. I got pregnant soon afterwards and yelled for help. My parents wanted me aborted; Tony's father agreed with them: I'd been horrified.

Yet soon after that I began to learn how to earn my living. Tony did that for me — you have the child and you accept that you have to provide. I'd managed, because I have a small talent for the design business. Life wasn't easy, but I managed. I thought I was in love a few times but nothing lasted, nothing mattered. I was hardened. But not invulnerable.

For the first time since Tony's father asked me to have an abortion as the price of his marrying me, I was absolutely desolated. A year without Richard? No, I'd yelled. I did the whole feminine thing, the yelling and the bawling, then the outrage.

Richard had been firm. The race was the culmination of his life's work. He said he was leaving in the morning for Monteine Castle to talk over the sponsorship International Marine Oil had offered. His yacht would fly International's house flag. If he won, they'd get marvellous publicity; and they were a large, generous combine. I told Richard they could have him.

I sulked when he left in the morning. He rang that evening, but I said the kind of stupid things that one is ashamed of even before they're out of one's mouth. He didn't ring Tuesday or Wednesday; on Thursday I panicked.

I'd intended visiting my Northern contacts — that's what I told Gloria, Tony's father's sister, who loves my boy as much as I do — and I rang around making appointments and began my Lincolnshire-Yorkshire-Cheshire-Lancashire circuit, which normally takes three days. I held out till Friday afternoon when I finished buying in Harrogate before setting off to see Richard.

When I saw him waving, I began to laugh aloud. The Fiat's tyres squealed as I braked.

'Anne!' he called again. 'I love you!'

I let out the clutch at once, the Fiat stalled and he had the car door open in a moment.

'If I hadn't seen the way you came along the drive I'd have said I was dreaming, Anne.' He flicked the seatbelt release and disengaged me from the straps. I was out of the car and in his arms without any effort on my part. He kissed me and I knew I'd wait a year or whatever he said.

'I tried to get in touch this morning, Anne — I didn't want to ring until I was fairly sure I'd do for the job.'

'Job!'

So far as I knew, Richard was visiting Monteine Castle to arrange some kind of sponsorship deal with a multinational oil combine. Richard was a good bet to win the Three Oceans Race and whatever happened they'd got their money's worth.

Over his shoulder I saw a tall blonde-haired woman of maybe forty-five or so regarding us with some interest. She pretended to be looking elsewhere when I caught her stare. There was something about her tiny smile that disturbed me. I pulled away.

'That woman's watching,' I said.

Richard turned. She walked towards us. 'Hello, Monica,' he said. 'Anne's here.'

I had been talked about. No woman likes it.

'I'm Monica Sievel,' the woman said.

She had been handsome once, but now her square, angular face looked ravaged. 'I work here.'

I put on my cool look. 'How do you do?'

I knew that I disliked and distrusted her intensely the moment I looked at her smoothly made-up face and saw the carefully guarded caution in her eyes.

This woman was inimical to me. I felt it, a skin thing, and I saw it in her eyes. She would do me harm. And Richard. He grinned at her.

'Monica's one of the staff — drinks like a fish and knows all my secrets. I was just telling Anne about the job — oh, I know it's unofficial!' he said, as she was about to interrupt. 'Nothing signed and sealed yet and I'm not to discuss it with anyone as Falco said, but Anne's special! She doesn't know it yet, but Ulrome's got her future planned. Come on, Anne, let's have a drink!' He stopped suddenly as he was pulling me along. 'Monica, the house-rules allow guests, don't they?'

Her charm and ability to handle any and every situation made a nonsense of my first reaction, She tucked her arm into Richard's and said that house-rules didn't exist at Monteine Castle.

'Richard's got to bring you to dinner,' she said firmly. 'One of the privileges of living in a castle is that occasionally one can act with an altogether aristocratic open-handedness. Anyway, International can afford it.'

I looked for a wedding ring, saw none and wondered why she hadn't married. I wondered if she was attractive to men, then immediately I thought of Richard without me for three days, and that wasn't a line of speculation I wanted to go into.

She had already gauged my feeling with an exact nicety that proved her intelligence, and set out to disarm me at once.

'He mentioned you,' she said. 'There had to be someone special.'

Even after her charming invitation I had the urge to grab Richard by the shoulders and push him hard into the car and drive off. Then I thought of Richard, and myself no longer alone, and the woman was so obviously good-natured and sincere that I told myself not to be a fool.

I looked at Monteine Castle again. It didn't look so forbidding, it gave an impression of strength and nobility. A few seagulls wheeled around the cliffs. The thick grey clouds were breaking up and I could see a patch of blue sky, miles away over the sea. A strong shaft of sunlight caught the towers, making a picturesque scene more vivid. Why had the Castle seemed menacing, in that one instant? It didn't now.

'It's kind of you,' I said, 'but I'd thought of staying in the village, There's a pub,' I said. I explained about the circuit. Tomorrow morning I'd go on to my two Lancashire artists, then motor through to Cheshire. I said I'd dropped in because I'd happened to find myself near; not much of an excuse, however one looked at it. 'Richard, I'm tired, why don't we go down and get a room for me?'

'But they've got guest rooms here! It's a marvellous setup — Monica, can you fix it?'

The woman's eyes were calculating

again, the warmth had gone. It was just a flicker but I thought I saw that glint of menace again. She recovered immediately.

'Of course!' she said. 'Why didn't I think of it — it's far too late for you to start worrying about a room at the Landing.'

I saw the look and didn't like what I saw.

I began to prepare my apologies, but Richard gave me no time. Besides, I was full of cautious elation, a good deal of curiosity, and just a touch of fury because Richard had given me such a bad time, leaving me to believe he'd come to Monteine Castle to fix the race sponsorship. He hustled me into the passenger seat. 'Anne, we'll have a large one to celebrate — in you get, Monica,' he said.

'No thanks, darlings — you drive on. I haven't had a breath of fresh air all day. It's rained non-stop. You two go ahead. I want a few minutes out here. If you go to the bar, I'll know where to find you a when I've arranged Anne's room. See you soon!'

She walked away and turned to the rear of the Castle.

Richard flicked through the gears and in seconds we were before a pair of iron-studded oak doors. Richard hadn't stopped talking — how wonderful the opportunity was, something about the Bahamas and interviews; but I was rather dazed. After all, I'd come to bitch at him and tell him that our relationship was over and by his choice. He was to have circumnavigated the globe. I thought I was inured to shock and found I wasn't.

Richard was about to hurl himself from the car.

'Wait,' I said. 'Sit there till you've answered my questions.'

'Yours to command,' said Richard. 'I could do with that drink, though — '

'Quiet! You didn't tell me about any job. Why not?'

'It's the Ulrome way, my love. I didn't want you to get too excited about the prospect.'

'You could have told me. What is this job anyway? And don't say it's going to keep us apart!'

'No chance,' he said. 'Would you believe it, International were looking for an adviser for their West Indies offshore concessions. They want someone who's got a practical knowledge of conditions in the Caribbean. Then there's the liaison aspect of the job. They want their man to know his way around Government circles. And, darling, it so happens that my extensive acquaintance includes half of the hoi polloi of Jamaica, Barbados, Trinidad, and the other, smaller islands, to say nothing of the Bahamas, which, by the way, is where International's Caribbean base is located. And, quite unofficially so they say, they've got their man. At a very high rate indeed. And how's that for a washed-up sailor with an overdraft few banks can afford?'

'But you wanted to sail! You wanted to do the three Oceans Race!'

'I wanted you too, Anne.'

'But you'd have to live there!'

'How do the Bahamas grab you?'

I thought of myself and Tony and Richard on a long white beach, the kind they show in the brochures. Unreality and dreams, I thought. Things had never gone right for me.

'You'd never be happy in a job like that.'

'I had to grow up sometime,' Richard said. 'The last of the Ulrome money's gone. Sponsorships aren't easy any more. Better sailors are getting the big combines to back them. I don't want to start taking seasick tourists out for weeks in the Med, and I'm damned if I'm going to smuggle cigarettes and the rest of it. I could be out of debt in six months, Anne. And I think I could be worth their money. Offshore drilling is a hazardous game. I know the waters like my own backyard. They won't be getting a bad bargain.'

'Let's get this straight,' I said, trying not to sound and look as delighted as I felt. 'You came here to be interviewed for a job in the Bahamas with the International Marine Oil Company, and they've offered you a job?'

'Not formally. Off the record, yes.'

'You told me you were going away for a year — '

Richard held me again. 'I thought

about it and decided I couldn't leave you.'

No woman I know could have been other than flattered, exhilarated and generally overwhelmed. Richard was *the* Richard Ulrome, the man whose name was synonymous with adventure, courage and the extremes of physical danger. I was the woman for whom he was giving up a chance of sailing in the longest single-handed race ever.

He grinned. Naturally he didn't remind me of my tantrum, but he couldn't help a slight dig at me. 'In a couple of minutes you're going to be telling me that you want me at sea. Before that happens, let's get you watered and fed. How does a Campari soda sound?'

I told myself I was a silly cow as we got out of the car. Nevertheless, I couldn't believe, deep down, that it would all come good for the two of us, not that easily.

'We'd have to get married,' he said.

I began to believe it all.

2

Someone with discrimination and great wealth had once owned Monteine Castle. The walls were smooth, probably not the original facing stone; but it was the local white-grey limestone of the cliffs, and beautifully finished. Two huge, brilliant tapestries showing eighteenth-century pastoral scenes hung on the long wall to the left of the porch. There were rows of prints and a couple of excellent oils that might have been Flemish — both were portraits of men in the style of Rubens.

The main staircase was a gorgeous early nineteenth-century ironwork masterpiece recently painted in a stark white, which set it off admirably against the exquisite tapestries. It wasn't a particularly large hall, but the proportions were excellent. Stone pillars flanked the interior of the doorway. There were several doorways at the back of the hall, and an open door to the right.

Richard let me look around. He was smiling smugly as I tried not to show how impressed I was by the lavish International setup. For everything spoke of the lavish use of money. I know about furnishings, and these looked like genuine Tudor pieces, heavy chests, high-back chairs, carved sideboards and cupboards; there was some nineteenth-century brass too. The best pieces were two huge highly ornate pitchers, one on each side of the fireplace.

There was even a fire, and I was glad of it since the day had begun to be chill. My respect for Richard's prospective employers grew as he dumped my overnight case and led me across the hall to the open door at the right of the splendid staircase.

'In here, my love,' he said.

I wanted to start asking Richard how he'd heard about the job. Then there were things like when would the offer be formal, how long would it take to complete his initial training, if any, what was expected of oil-company executives' wives, and how Tony was going to be explained away.

But when I saw the small but well-stocked bar and the elegant little lounge, all I could think of saying was, 'If I'm staying over, I'll have to cancel my morning appointments, Richard.'

'Good evening, Madam — Sir,' a deferential and deep voice said behind me.

I started, for I hadn't noticed anyone. I saw a dark-haired, heavily-built, middle-aged man in the uniform of the posher kind of cocktail lounge.

'Max,' said Richard. 'Max is the steward,' he told me. 'This is Miss Blackwell. We'll have Campari sodas, easy on the ice, a twist of lemon in each and some black olives. We'll be having dinner. Anything special on the menu tonight?'

'The pheasant would be your best choice, Sir,' said Max.

He wasn't English-born. There was no recognizable accent. Slav, I thought, with that heavy face and square build. His eyes were brilliant — black and shiny as chunks of pitch.

'The pheasant, then,' said Richard. 'And, by the way, I'd like to make a call or two. What time was the appointment for, Anne?'

He was arranging things for me, and I was glad of it. I'd been driving for quite a time, and I was tired.

'Perhaps I could make any necessary arrangements?' suggested Max.

I began to realize how important Richard must be to International. The whole establishment seemed to revolve around the man in my life.

'I can make the call,' I said. 'If you'll pass me the phone?'

'Of course, Madam.'

With a little gesture of his hands and a small bow, Max indicated that he approved of my show of independence. He was so deferential it annoyed me.

I delayed my appointment with some brusqueness and finished two more drinks in rapid order. I began to feel uneasy. There had been too many surprises in too short a time. Richard saw that I was thoroughly upset.

'Dinner's in about half-an-hour,' he said. 'Monica, what room have you put Anne in?'

I hadn't noticed the big blonde woman entering.

'Do let me show you, dear,' she said at once. 'Or would you take Anne to her room, Richard? It's on the same floor as yours. The Yellow Room,' To me she said: 'The Chairman likes to keep to the old traditions, and that's what the room has always been called, the Yellow Room. Absolutely no ghosts or nastiness, I assure you, dear. And every comfort. We're modelled on Hilton standards here at Monteine. International are absolutely filthy with money, and why not, the prices they charge for petrol! But don't let me keep you — Richard will show you how everything works.'

'Then that's all settled,' he said. 'Thanks, Monica. The Yellow Room it is. No, I'll take the case, Max,' he said to the bar-steward.

Max bowed. The Camparis went to my head about then and I felt the delicious lightness that comes when someone else is taking charge and you have no more need to make decisions.

The Castle was a strange old place.

Rooms led to more corridors, sometimes up a flight of stairs, sometimes down a couple of flights. I thought it was marvellous. We passed up the splendid staircase, through a sort of smallish lounge littered with papers and magazines; then up a narrow, winding passage to another room, with a blazing log fire in a brick fireplace.

I liked the room immediately. It looked incredibly old; the brick was toned by age to a mellow red-gold almost the colour of the flames from the hawthorn logs. I asked Richard to stop whilst I looked around it, then I pulled him over to a wide, mullioned window from which I could see clear across the sweep of the cliffs and, beyond, to the sea six hundred feet below.

The room was a sort of workplace with a couple of writing desks and rows of leather-bound books along one wall, and lots of pictures, pictures on all the other walls. There were rows of prints all of one family. I glanced at one Italian face. The man was a Venetian called Enrico Capelli. He had died in 1462. I reflected that he looked like the younger Nixon, stubbly-dark and amiable, but with a hint of the cunning to come.

'Up here,' said Richard, pointing out another opening through gorgeous red velvet curtains.

Again we were in a corridor, much narrower, which led upwards to one wing of the castle. There was a rounded roof that looked as if it might be the original stonework.

Eventually we reached a fairly short corridor. There were two doors.

'Yours,' said Richard, stopping at a small-ish, heavy oak door. 'Mind your head.'

They must have been shorter in the Middle Ages, for I had to stoop to get into the room.

'And the step,' said Richard.

I stepped down onto thick carpet and saw one of the most attractive rooms I've ever been in. It was small, with stone walls and a fairly low ceiling; yet though it should have seemed cold and even damp, that wasn't the feeling I had. The carpet was thick Wilton, a dusky sort of gold, and the furniture mid-Victorian, all delicate mahogany with gold-patterned inlays. A small window gave enough light; I looked out and again I could see the long, slow grey waves of the North Sea.

Richard put the case down and pointed out the television set, the tiny bathroom and the telephone for room service.

'It's so pretty!' I said. 'I hate antiquey rooms stuffed with bits of junk, but this seems so right.'

Richard murmured agreement and ran his hand along my back.

'Whoever fitted this place out was an artist,' I said. 'And stop that, or I can't talk. You haven't started to tell me anything about International. How did you hear about the job?'

Richard sighed. 'It was all so easy, really. It was a couple of weeks back. I met a fellow I know vaguely and we said how are things, then the talk got around to jobs — then I saw the advertisement, and we talked about it. After a few drinks it seemed a good idea if I rang through.'

'Just like that?'

'That's how International work, apparently. You call them and if they like you they send for you to be evaluated.'

'To Monteine Castle? Just like that?'

'Oh no. Interviews in London first, then a meeting with the British directors. After that they said I'd need to be vetted by their tame headshrinkers.'

'So you rang them?' I prompted.

'They said I probably fitted the bill at the interview.'

'And they told you to come here? It's more like a hotel than a set of offices.'

'That's where they're so subtle, Anne,' yawned Richard. 'They watch you. You'll see, love. When we go down to dinner, you'll meet the rest of the team — the headshrinkers. Don't you know how they operate?'

I'd heard something of selection procedures, but I'd never had occasion to be involved at this level before.

'Tell me,' I said.

'Falco Jensen, Eric Fitch and Monica,' he said. 'They've so much brain between them they're top-heavy. And they watch, Anne, by God they watch!'

I looked around as he said it, and for a moment I had a return of that unpleasant, bewildering sensation I had experienced when I first caught sight of Monteine Castle.

I had to examine the room to see if anyone was watching. It sounds crazy, but I was sure that there was another presence in the room.

'Now what?' asked Richard, as I padded about the clinging carpet.

'You know how I am about strange rooms.'

I opened the wardrobe and looked under the bed. I pushed aside a sliding door in a cabinet, and saw a smooth blank screen.

'Every comfort,' said Richard. He showed me the recess behind the bed-head board. 'Any strange men?'

'All right, I'm a fool,' I apologized. I didn't want to spoil his pleasure, for he was pleased about the job.

'It can be a bit creepy in the dark,' he said. 'And along the cliffs at night you sometimes get the feeling that you're at the end of the world. It's as lonely out here as anything I've known at sea. There's something about the cliffs at night that's positively eerie.'

I shivered and went to the window again. I didn't want to know about the cliffs at night. In the gathering gloom of evening, the sea had a slow and surging emptiness that was disturbing. I turned back to Richard.

'Who's Monica Sievel?'

'Monica's an expert on psychotic traumas, so Falco tells me. I can't tell you much about him, but I've heard of this character Fitch before, and I know for a fact that he's an expert in his field. But you'll see them soon — and be seen, Anne,' he warned. 'Oh, there's no secret about it, old girl,' he said, laughing. He had noticed that I didn't like the idea at all.

'Look, stop being so serious about it all! They have to compare notes about my reactions to everyday events — they showed me the charts they make up. Everything goes down, the way I walk, the things I say when they ask me questions, the way I begin a conversation, what I eat, how I dress, everything. I bet they're talking over your arrival right now, Anne.

It's the way they work,' he insisted as I began to say how much I disliked the idea of being on trial. 'Look, it's a joke, Anne. It really is funny!'

'All right, it's funny — so long as you get the job.'

'It's in the bag!'

'Well, that's all right.'

It wasn't, of course.

'A couple of gins will put you right, love. Let the shrinks look into our souls — they've nothing better to do so we might as well let them have their fun.'

'You go down,' I said. 'I know the way.'

It sounded absurd but I didn't want to appear before the staff at Monteine Castle arm in arm with Richard, as if we were a married couple.

Richard waited a moment.

'I'm getting a shower — I'll be half an hour. Don't drink too much.'

After Richard left I took time over my toilet. Then I made my way downstairs

I had no trouble in finding my way through the corridors and passages until I came to the working-lounge which served as a sitting room and library, and then I must have taken a wrong turning, for instead of passing through the arched passageway which led to the imposing iron-work stairway, somehow I found myself in a dark, narrow, brick-lined tunnel, which wound downwards very steeply.

I had to be very careful, since I was wearing a pair of high diamanté-starred sandals without backs. I knew I'd gone wrong after I'd descended about the height of two storeys, which put me somewhere near ground level. However, there was no sign that the passageway gave on to the ground floor, so I thought I'd better turn back.

There were small, narrow windows. I could see recessed lights, but I hadn't found a switch and the windows were too high for me to see out of them. But the slits let in a little light, quite enough to see by, and if it hadn't been for the wretched sandals I would have been fine. As it was, I missed a rather worn step on a sharp turn and twisted sideways, banging my arm sharply on the brick-work. I clutched at the wall, and twisted on the high heels.

The air whooshed out of my lungs, I teetered crazily for a moment or two and then somehow recovered my balance, but my right ankle had been badly wrenched. I had to sit down after that to get my breath back and to clear the tears from my eyes.

I wanted to yell out for help, and I suppose if I'd been in any other situation I would have done just that, but it seemed so ludicrous that a grown woman should first have missed her way and then her footing. I felt I should make a complete fool of myself in front of prying strangers who would be only too happy to score a few points in their notebooks.

My head cleared after a minute or two, and the pain became tolerable. When I tried to put the foot to the floor I knew the damage wasn't serious. So I got to my feet and I turned back.

I had gone up two steps before it occurred to me that I was a diamanté sandal short. I went down again and, now that my sight was accustomed to the semi-darkness, I saw what I had missed before, a doorway.

It was around the next bend, and my sandal gleamed as a few rays of light came through the warped panels of a wooden door. I stepped down with great care onto the wrenched foot and at once heard the sound of voices.

'She could be a thorough nuisance, I'm sorry,' someone was saying over a murmur of protest. I knew the voice. It was the woman who had invited me to stay at Monteine Castle, Monica Sievel. One of the other voices had me puzzled, for I had heard it before, and recently at that; instinctively I stopped. 'I know about the degree of control the woman exerts,' the man's voice went on. 'She's an aggressive and assertive personality, but that isn't necessarily an adverse factor. Now that the New York operation is complete, we move on to the critical stage. Ulrome may well need her support. Why not involve her at the beginning. It can't be kept from her — and we can't arrange another major settlement. I think we have to keep this in perspective. She could even prove a catalyst in this situation. Fitch, what's your reading of her state of mind?'

I was listening to a conversation about myself and Richard. I felt cold at the thought. I had no qualms at all about eavesdropping. If others talk about me, then I have the right to listen in. The thought that was uppermost in my mind was the damage I might do to Richard's new career if they found me listening. Had they heard me? Or had they heard the tumble down the stairs?

'Aggressive. Assertive. Yet herself an unrealized psyche,' said another man. I almost decided to retreat silently but I stayed to hear more. An effeminate man's voice was answering, talking about me. I strained to hear his voice, but he was talking so quietly that I missed whole sequences. I caught the words: 'She had for some time a considerable drug dependency. She won't revert. I'd estimate that right up to the final stage she'd hold up. Why *not* use her?'

I could have screamed with anger. They knew about the trips I'd been on when I was with Tony's father. There wasn't much else, no hard drugs, no real addiction, and I was seventeen at the time. I tried to remember what 'catalyst' meant. *Catalyst?* I was that? And I was to be *used?*

'Strategy, Jensen?' said the calm authoritative voice I has almost placed.

'My report, page seven,' said another man, a deep bass. 'I see no reason to change it in any way. I had anticipated the possibility of the woman's presence.'

I heard the murmur of voices and the sound of papers rustling. I shuddered. I knew now what I had only suspected when I saw the Sievel woman regarding me with that curious stare. She was inimical to me. And so were her colleagues. They were setting me up for something, and it involved Richard's welfare; in my innocence I thought they were engaged in some scheme to separate me from him because they thought I wasn't a suitable International Marine Oil Company wife. I told myself to keep it cool. No confrontations, no anger. I wouldn't let Richard down. I retrieved my sandal stealthily and made my way back.

I plastered my arm, rubbed some of my most expensive perfume on the ankle, and took out my third-best dress, a long-sleeved two-year-old cotton thing, mostly red, but shot through with Chinese silks. Then I went downstairs again.

'You took your time, Anne,' Richard remarked.

He must have been drinking steadily, for he was flushed. Monica Sievel smiled at me, and I thought, *You deceitful cow*. Two other men were there: one was a short, slight, nearly bald middle-aged man; the other was rather older, maybe in his late fifties and massively built with a huge paunch and great red jowls. He was Jensen, as I expected. His deep, plummy voice matched his bulk. Fitch was the possessor of the effeminate voice I had heard describe me as aggressive and assertive. Richard introduced me to them. I felt myself flushing. They must know that I had been listening to them: surely? But they gave no sign of it,

They asked me about my journey, how did I like the Castle, did I know North Yorkshire — all the usual things. Jensen suggested a drink for me.

'What will you have, Miss Blackwell?' the bar-steward asked me.

I staggered, literally. I put the hurt foot down and had to grab at Richard's arm for support. Pain lanced through my leg, and a sudden chill struck back through the whole of my body.

It was the way he said my name that brought back the memory of that decisive, so-calm voice that I had over-heard; whilst I was eavesdropping I couldn't give any credence to the possibility. A bar-steward giving orders? Impossible. The impossible had happened, but why — why was an intelligent man like him masquerading as a servant?

'Here, Anne, what's the matter?' Richard asked.

Concern registered also on the woman's face. I thought I could conceal my feelings. I couldn't. She held my gaze and then came forward in a motherly way.

'Is it your foot? See — it's swelling!'

Richard inspected my ankle and the barman made sympathetic noises. I tried to avoid looking behind the bar in case they knew I would be looking for the folder they had been reading. I had an absurd impulse to say 'It's all on page seven', but I kept it back.

'I slipped in the shower,' I told them. 'On a piece of soap.'

Fitch smiled and then looked away. Jensen put his fingers on my shoulder and I managed to restrain the shudder I felt beginning in my spine.

'A drink might help,' suggested Max.

I couldn't answer him for a moment. He knew so much about me. And then it struck me why he should choose to work as a bar-steward; he was in the ideal position to watch. Almost unnoticed, he could spy on International guests and record their unguarded words. It was clever. I resolved to be very careful.

'Maybe you feel sick,' said Richard. 'Here, shall we give dinner a miss? Have a sandwich and a glass of wine upstairs?'

I smiled at them all. I slid onto a barstool and called on my store of confidence, though I felt like a sixteen-year-old bride. I looked at the man with the calm, authoritative voice.

'A very large gin,' I told him.

Had I known of the seismic changes that were soon to undermine our lives, I would have taken more than the one large measure of spirits.

3

The dinner was a disaster.

I was on the defensive from the moment a neat little waiter appeared to tell us it was ready. I knew what to expect, for I had looked up the word 'catalyst' in the library on my way down to the bar. I was, as the dictionary put it, a substance that causes change. I was part of an experiment.

They were going to watch the effects of my presence on Richard: I was sure that they would try to needle me into committing some social gaffe that would then reveal me as unsuitable for an International executive's wife.

Mercifully, Max was out of earshot. He stayed in the bar, making a pretence of deferring to the three, Jensen, Fitch and the Sievel woman as the waiter ushered us through the entrance hall of Monteine Castle to a large dining room.

I wobbled on my sandals, but I didn't

wince. Richard made me lean on his arm, and Jensen solicitously placed his large fat hand under my right elbow. I couldn't help glancing back as we passed into the panelled room. The pseudo-barman was watching me. I might have been a laboratory specimen for all the humanity he showed.

'Madam,' said the waiter, helping me into an antique tall-back chair. I sat down and smiled at the Sievel woman. She would attack first.

'I've done it myself,' she smiled back. 'The soap,' she explained. 'I've slipped on my butt before now. So undignified! And it hurts!'

Fitch poured the wine. 'I can't imagine Miss Blackwell in any but a dignified position.'

Jensen said, 'Do let's stop embarrassing Anne and decide what we wish for the first course of this excellent meal. The game pâté is superb with the Pommard!'

'Richard's told us a little about your work, Anne,' said Eric Fitch, when all but Richard had chosen the pâté. 'Does it involve a great deal of travelling?'

I caught the faint whiff of some form of perfume from him as he handed me the päté. I disliked him intensely from that moment.

'Goes with the job, doesn't it, darling,' said Richard. 'Anne's a good driver.'

'I'd say that Anne would be very competent at whatever she put her hand to,' said Jensen, dipping his toast and päté into a glass of green wine. He sniffed at the result.

Eric Fitch laughed. 'It's quite a cut-throat business, the design world, so I hear. And you've prospered. Falco's right. You must be very competent.'

'How did you start, Anne?' asked Monica Sievel,

They knew, of course. They'd investigated me thoroughly, but I mustn't show that I knew.

'I could always draw and paint a little,' I said. 'I realized my limitations at about sixteen, though. I knew I wasn't good enough for original work, but I could match materials and design. I freelanced and I was lucky in getting some good, reliable artists.'

'So you're an artistic entrepreneur,' smiled Fitch. 'How clever you must be.'

He was mocking me. I kept my temper. Richard took their interest for what it seemed to be: polite, easy flattery.

'It's more of an instinct for sensing what fits the mood of the times,' I said, and drank some wine.

'Your Anne has a marvellous life,' said Monica in her deep, sincere tones. 'You've no idea what a bore it can be, the endless round of personality tests on people who are far more interesting than oneself. Lucky girl,' she smiled.

'Terrible bore,' agreed Jensen, as he finished his wine. 'Look at Richard. Full of health. Enough action and excitement behind him to fill a dozen lives. Unlimited prospects before him — '

'Depending on your reports,' Richard pointed out. 'I haven't officially been offered a job yet, and I've yet to consider the offer if and when it comes.'

'Outspoken and crisp,' said Eric Fitch.

It was coming. I sensed it in the slight edge of malice in Fitch's tone, 'And with the finest prospects a man could wish for in this age,' said Jensen, unperturbed by Richard's interruption. 'Everything about Richard says he's a notable acquisition for the company.'

'Of course!' I burst out.

'Steady on the wine,' said Richard very quietly, for I was on my second glass of the green-white wine by now. I hadn't noticed that the waiter had refilled my glass.

'You're both lucky,' said Jensen. 'A meeting of the talents. Embodied in the male, strength and courage. And, if it isn't too fanciful, in the lady here, all the qualities of creativeness and beauty that best complement the man of action. Ah, the pheasant!'

The little waiter made quite a business of removing the cover of the huge platter. There were six pheasants, neatly arrayed two by two, cock and hen together. I might have felt hungry if I hadn't been so apprehensive. The carving and the serving took long enough for me to recover my composure, and Richard and I were able to take a little time out to talk about ordinary things. He asked about Tony. I said he wasn't expecting me till the weekend. I asked if there were any other guests at the Castle; there weren't. Then I wanted to whisper that I had overheard the bar-steward and the others, but I sensed an alertness as they made jokes about one another's appetites; without seeming to, they were listening. When Jensen took the carver and flicked it around the steel, I felt he was about to dissect me. I took the recommended portion.

Red wine was poured, dark-red and beautiful in the cut-glass goblets.

Fitch neatly chomped his way through the large plateful of food before him; Jensen guzzled noisily, doing a Falstaff act. Monica Sievel began to draw Richard out in conversation. She asked about simple things, beginning with food at sea. I listened carefully, but they all seemed to have forgotten about me,

Richard explained that the storage space on his latest yacht was enough for a complete range of frozen and dehydrated foods. He was enjoying himself thoroughly; he loves talking about boats.

I began to unwind, thankful that I had been ignored. Richard finished telling quite an amusing story about cooking a Christmas dinner for himself in a Force Seven gale along the coast of South-West Africa, when Monica Sievel turned to me and said:

'You'll have to get Richard to write it all down for your children, my dear!'

'Children?' I said, and noticed that my glass had been filled again. Fitch was watching me.

'I made a few notes of my voyages,' Richard said. 'A sort of extended log, but I wouldn't know how to make stories of them. Not my line of country at all.'

He didn't know that the Sievel woman was needling me about my son.

'Richard's often told my son about his experiences,' I said, very deliberately. 'Tony would keep Richard telling stories for hours at bedtimes if I let him, wouldn't he, Richard?'

Richard was quite unaware of the byplay. 'Little beggar,' he said. 'As a matter of fact, he made me promise him I'd take him along to Burnham. She's in the boatyard now,' he explained to the others. 'I wanted a couple of modifications to the line of the keel. I don't suppose Tony told you about it, love?'

'Just before I came away.'

Now I feared they would begin to probe into my early adult life and bring out the fact that I hadn't been married to Tony's father.

I realized that I was losing my cool, for my cheeks burned.

But it didn't happen. Instead, Eric Fitch said, 'You haven't had any of the sauce!'

'No.'

I caught the whiff of perfume again. Estee Lauder. A friend of mine used it.

Richard helped me to the sauce, though I could cheerfully have hurled my plate and its contents at the effeminate little man beside me. Fitch and the Sievel woman would go for me now.

'I can't think when I've had a better meal,' Richard said appreciatively. 'What do you say, Anne?'

He knew I was distraught, but I think he had put it down to the hurt ankle.

'Anne's not feeling too well, are you?' said the Sievel woman. 'Stop filling her glass,' she told Eric Fitch, who was pouring more of the heavy red wine into my glass. 'She's a working girl and she's obviously had a long day.'

'It's a marvellous meal,' I said. 'And I'd enjoy another glass of the burgundy.' I was at the stage where I would do exactly the opposite of what anyone suggested.

'I like to see women eating well. And drinking,' said Fitch. 'That's the charm of primitive communities, you know. I was commissioned to do a study of aboriginal eating customs a couple of years back. One of the big American philanthropic trusts put up the money. Go and research their food fetishes, they commanded. And I went. Extraordinary people. Odd customs.'

'Don't be mysterious, Eric,' reproved the Sievel woman. 'The aboriginals. Come on, what was odd about them?'

'Nothing to do with their food — a boring diet. It happened whilst I was at a small town in the interior, a quite horrid experience. The local traders knew I was interested in the aboriginals' customs, and they knew too that I was some sort of scientist.'

Fitch smiled.

'I saw a dead man speak.'

It should have been shocking or at least have produced a dramatic effect, but it didn't shock or awe me.

I exploded with laughter into the long silence that followed his announcement. Red wine sprayed over the tablecloth. I gulped and gasped for air, and began to laugh aloud. As I spluttered and howled, I turned to Richard and saw an expression of shock on his face, and I knew that at last I had done what the three interrogators wished. I had offended him.

Richard used his napkin to help me tidy up, and the waiter appeared with fresh table linen. To cover my embarrassment the other three began a conversation about similar occurrences in their lives.

'All right now?' asked Richard, when I had recovered. 'Must have gone down the wrong way,' he said quietly. 'Eric, what were you saying?'

'It wasn't much of a story,' Fitch said.

'Nothing more than an apparently super-natural manifestation which could be rationalized by anyone with a minimum of scientific training.'

I felt that I had to say something, in case Richard believed me to be insensitive.

'What was the explanation for your dead aboriginal's continued speechifying?'

'It was all to do with air pressure,' he replied. 'In itself quite a remarkable phenomenon. You see, the dead man was kept perfectly preserved m the desert air. He had been buried, though that isn't the right term for it — for they used a stilted platform for their dead — in a small depression in the desert where the evening winds coming down from two mountain ranges met at sundown. A small amount of air which had expanded during the heat of the day became cooler and passed through his vocal cords.' He paused. 'Yet the whole tribe believes he is one of the living dead.'

The room was very quiet. I couldn't see a pattern in the way the conversation was leading. There was a disturbing undercur-rent of connivance in the glances of the three International psychologists.

'Nonsense, Eric,' said the Sievel woman. She indicated the remains on her plate. 'Once physical death occurs, there's nothing left but the bones. The trouble with you field-workers is that you adopt the superstitions of the communities you meet. But men are the dreamers, aren't they, Anne?'

I didn't want any more talk about dead men speaking.

'Richard's as down-to-earth as any man I've known,' I said.

'Andre,' said Jensen, gesturing largely at the waiter, who then cleared the table with his neat unobtrusive skill. 'So, no mysteries for you, Richard? But I thought the sea was the last home for romantics and visionaries. No stories for us, Richard? No experiences that left you with the feeling that you thought there were some answers you didn't want to find in your charts?'

Andre, neat as a bird, brought on a selection of sweets as Richard considered. Then:

'I've had the usual hallucinations,' he

said. 'I've seen all the mythical beings when I've been short on food and sleep. The fruit,' he told Andre. 'But it was always hallucinatory. As for anything approaching Eric's tale, no.'

'But there was something?' prompted Monica Sievel, her voice soothing and confidential.

'I've never told anyone before,' Richard said slowly. 'I'd not seen a living soul for over a month, and then it was only a little cargo boat. Nothing after that for days. I was right off the main lanes, more or less idling, trying out a new rig for an Australian manufacturer. I'd been for a swim, with a line, of course, and I'll swear the sea was empty when I went over the side.'

'I saw a fishing-boat whilst I was in the water,' he went on. 'The boards were bleached white and streaked by drying weeds. The hull was high in the water, as though she was out of ballast. I couldn't see more than her boards and her single mast — not her people, not her upper works. I remember the pleasure I felt in the end of my loneliness. I pulled myself back to the yacht and began waving as I climbed up the side,'

Richard's handsome face looked tired. I felt the weight of his loneliness, and the mystery he had kept to himself.

'I could see the remains of a sail — the usual island rig for that part of the world. And the baskets they use for their catch.'

'And?' prompted Jensen.

'The crew.' Richard stabbed with a fruit fork at the guavas on his plate. The waiter deftly removed the wine glasses and brought on two bottles of a German wine. 'Dead, of course. The bizarre thing was that they were all in position. One man at the tiller. Another in the bows looking forward as if he could see his landfall. There was one other, and he had his back to the small cabin amidships, for all the world as though he'd been on watch all night and it was his turn to loll back whilst the others sailed the boat. I shouted to them even as I realized that they had been dead for months, for every man was dried and withered by sun and spray. Their faces and limbs were crusted so white they looked like stone men. God knows how they'd died, and so much at their ease.'

I stared at Richard, wishing I could say something that would break the heavy silence.

4

We know — usually long afterwards — that there is a moment when we should have intervened. It passes, and this one passed, quite unrecognized.

After a while, Richard went on:

'I could have followed the boat, wherever it was going. It would have been an easy matter to board her and examine her dead crew.'

'Who says there are no mysteries?' said Fitch, pouring out the sweet, delicious wine for himself, and then for the rest of us.

'You never reported this, did you, Richard?' said Monica Sievel.

'No.'

'And you didn't board the boat?' asked Jensen.

'No more than I'd open a grave.'

'What a fantastic story,' said Eric Fitch. 'What an absolutely incredible story!'

'Neither fantastic nor incredible, Richard,'

said Jensen. 'Within the bounds of possibility, and entirely believable.'

'I was thinking the same thing,' said Monica Sievel. 'But Anne's getting bored with us — don't drink the stuff if you don't want it, dear.'

I swallowed my second glass of the fragrant sweet wine. I was becoming reckless.

'Were you anywhere in the Atlantic when you saw the boat?' I said to Richard, 'Not anywhere near New York, darling?'

New York. I wanted them to hear me say it, to know that I had heard what they were talking about. I watched their faces. Jensen, with his white, larded features; Fitch, his bald head shining with sweat; the Sievel woman and her constant smile. There was something about New York, and I had altogether forgotten what it was.

'No, my love,' said Richard. 'The New Hebrides belong to another world.'

Richard was still thinking of that remote sea and the salt-streaked hull, and it dismayed me to think that he was so far away from me. I looked around the three faces, the smooth, plastered face of the Sievel woman, with her impenetrable calm and her false smile; at Jensen, sweating and ironical; and at the contemptible Fitch, who was again pressing wine on me. New York, I had said, and not a sign that it meant anything to any of them; there was no response at all. I looked from one face to another, thinking all the while of my cleverness.

Surely they had heard me mention New York? Suddenly I felt cold. I had been reckless, and now, for no reason I could explain to myself, I knew fear.

Before I could begin to think of some way of diverting their attention from my deliberate mention of what I had overheard, Jensen spoke again.

'Richard, forgive me if I ask you this, but have you experienced a similar sense of wonder at any other time in your life?'

Richard gave the question some thought. Finally, he shook his head.

'No,' he said. 'I've had the kind of half-awake sensations I've mentioned, but they can be accounted for in purely physiological terms.' He smiled at me and pressed my hand.

Eric Pitch said into the quietness:

'Have you seen the sea break over the cliffs below, Richard?'

Before he could answer, the Sievel woman went on:

'I wouldn't like to be caught walking when the tide sweeps in — not nice at all!'

Jensen looked annoyed at the interruption.

'I suppose we sound parochial, Richard — there's nothing like the kind of conditions you've experienced?'

'There aren't many seas worse than the North Sea,' Richard said. 'I know that. A hundred-foot wave hit a rig out in the Brent oilfield a year back. I lost a good friend in that disaster.'

'It's a strange coast,' said Fitch slowly. 'I've talked to the locals and they'll tell you of waves like living things.'

'For God's sake — ' I began, for I hated the way the conversation was now turning.

Eric Fitch handed me my glass before I

could continue. His slightly bulbous eyes drilled straight at me.

'You've seen the waves break below the cliffs, haven't you, Anne?' he asked. 'Haven't you?'

'No,' I said. 'And I don't want to.'

'You should,' said Monica Sievel, laughing. 'I think there's nothing more agreeable than being high above the rocks and the cliffs and seeing the dark water swirling below — and all the time one's safely above it all, and the water and the rocks are there but they can't *harm*! Isn't that the point of it all?'

'And then looking back at the Castle!' Jensen rumbled. 'I think nothing can be more reassuring than the sight of the twin towers — you are in the South Tower, aren't you, Anne? — from the cliffs! Why, it's so exhilarating I've a mind to see it for myself later. Waves like monsters. You know, I can't help feeling we're straying into some odd territory.'

This was something new. I felt fear again.

'Then why talk about it?' I heard myself saying.

Jensen looked at me intently. 'But why talk about anything?' he asked. 'Why not talk about the local legends, since we're all here, and none of us with any particular acquaintance with the North Yorkshire coast? But of course if you'd rather talk about — '

'Anne's tired,' Richard said again.

He tried to pat my hand, but I blazed out:

'Don't fuss, Richard!'

'Go for a walk if you need a breath of fresh air,' said Fitch. 'Look at the waves and the sea.'

My head was swimming.

The Sievel woman smiled at Richard. 'Yes, go for a walk to the old chapel.'

Richard seemed in the grip of some curiously deadening emotion. I felt he was becoming remote from me as he looked at the Sievel woman.

'What chapel?' he asked quietly.

'Why, it's only half a mile along the headland.' Jensen put in. 'Surely you saw the track down the valley? Didn't we tell you about the old chapel? Of course, it's all bricked up now. Weird old place. Odd tales about it too.' He rolled liqueur around his glass. 'That is, if you're prepared to believe the stories of the local half-wits.'

'No, you didn't tell me anything about it. Not the chapel. Nor any tales,' said Richard.

I began to feel affected by the drink I'd had. It was beginning to drape a blanket on the unpleasant memories and converting my gaffes into triumphs.

'Tell me,' I said. 'I like weird places and stories.'

'Certainly not!' Monica Sievel said, smiling confidentially at me. 'Why you have to experience it for yourself — go and catch the mood. There's moonlight and the cliffs and the darkness below — and the ruined chapel! Go and catch your own ghosts, Anne.'

'A walk would do you both good,' Jensen assured us.

'You can't miss the track,' Fitch smiled. His wet eyes hypnotized me. 'Go right up to the chapel, Anne. Take Richard.'

I looked at Richard. He swayed slightly in his tall-backed chair. I didn't know what I wanted.

'Superb meal,' he said. 'Like to walk in the moonlight, love?'

'If you like.'

'Excuse me,' Richard said, dropping his cigar into a bowl of trifle. He didn't notice the way it hissed out, but I giggled as I saw the expression on the faces of Jensen, the Sievel woman and Fitch.

I basked in their approval.

'Wait until we're out of the room before you talk about us,' I said. What an exit line. I felt like a Bogart heroine.

I could hear them chuckling and murmuring appreciatively at my parting joke as we walked through the small bar and out into the entrance hall of Monteine Castle.

With a drunken clarity, I knew the evening was a disaster, but what pained in a dull and bitter way was that I did not know why; I knew, however, with an iron certainty, that whatever the evening brought would affect me immediately and dreadfully, and would go on winding its way into the fabric of my life with Richard, always threatening to destroy us.

5

I hardly noticed my swollen ankle until we were walking on the North side of the Castle. Richard caught me as I stumbled on a smooth piece of bedrock jutting out from the gravelled path.

'Damn them!'

I was sobering fast, becoming more aware of what I was doing.

'Richard, why don't we get out of it?'

He wasn't really listening.

'Of course, love.'

I was slowing, but Richard had me firmly by the arm. I said loudly:

'Richard, they were talking about you — and about me! Before the dinner, I mean. And that barman seemed to be the top man. Richard, slow down!'

But he was intent on the faint ribbon of pathway marked off from the lighter nightshades of grass and nettles and thistles by the occasional gleam of white rock.

'Oh, your ankle! I'm sorry — yes, lean on me.' He looked down at me for the first time since we had left the grounds of the Castle. I could see the blackness of the sea and a great swathe of moonlit waves crawling in the blackness beyond the cliff's edge. Richard's face was without a flicker of expression, either of concern for me or appreciation of my distress.

'The chapel isn't far,' he said.

'Damn the chapel!'

He stopped. And still he was staring along the cliff edge, towards a deep gash in the cliffs, about a quarter of a mile away. I took his face in my hands and made him look at me.

'I said they were talking about us,' I told him. 'The Sievel woman. And Jensen and Fitch. And Max, the bar-steward.'

He smiled at me. 'Why shouldn't they? Anne, that's what they're employed to do, love.'

'They didn't know I was listening. They knew all about me.' My head was spinning with the effort of concentration.

Over Richard's shoulder, I saw the

towers of the Castle outlined against the high moonlit clouds. I made out the twin lights of our adjoining rooms and wished I was safely inside with the warmth of Richard near me. 'I don't like them, and I don't like this place!'

'I'm not sure I like them either,' he said abstractedly. 'Why don't you and I stagger on a few paces and clear the cobwebs?'

He was moving as he said it.

'I'd rather go to bed.'

'Bed?' he said. 'Don't think I could sleep yet.'

'I'd rather find a hotel room,' I said. 'But I'll settle for anything at the moment.'

'Mind your step,' Richard said. It wasn't as far as I thought to the ravine-like valley. He propelled me gently down a fairly steep decline.

'Monica's right about this place,' he said.

I could make it out, now that my night vision was coming. Richard had eyes like a cat. He had already seen the ruins halfway down the side of the ravine. There was a fairly wide path, overgrown though. And a wooden gate barred the way.

'That's the chapel they were talking about?' I asked, for I couldn't help but be interested. There was a certain fascination about the scene: the white glare of the moonlight, the racing clouds, the tumbled masonry and the shape of the chapel itself: it was built partly on a ledge of rock and partly into the side of the ravine. Enough of it was standing to show that it had once been a substantial building.

'Yes. Let's take a look.'

Richard was fascinated too. There was an air of excitement about him, and a smile on his lips that gave him a cruel look. I had never seen him like this before. He pushed on the gate. It swung open easily enough.

'My ankle's hurting,' I said. He didn't hear my objection.

'The main body of the place has fallen in, but there's part of an arch still standing,' he said as he pulled me along. 'See, Anne. You know dates and things — what about the arch?'

'Oh, damn the arch!' I said. 'I've been

trying to tell you I don't like it here, not any of it, not the bloody Castle, nor the creeps back there! Richard, they're manipulating us! What do they want from us?'

Richard was smiling, but not at me.

'Jensen's bunch? All those headshrinker types get a kick out of the feeling they're in charge of someone or something. How about the arch?'

I couldn't make any impression on him.

Richard wasn't listening to me. So I looked again at the arch.

'The keystones make it probably sixteenth century,' I said. 'I could tell you more in the morning.'

He was staring at the brickwork. 'That would be about right,' he said quietly.

He had turned towards the sea. I could see the line of the breakers sweeping up the channel. I shivered, for there was a chill wind.

'About right for what?' I asked.

'Hmmm?' The faint, cruel smile was replaced by a look of puzzlement.

'Richard, what's troubling you?'

Something was, of that I was certain. I could feel the tension of his grip. Suddenly I was afraid again. The moonlight was stronger. I could fancy that the shadows moved in the harsh moonlight, and that the noises which I knew to be made by the cold night wind sighing through the tumbled walls were something much more sinister. I thought again of Monteine Castle's grey bulk as I had first seen it, outlined against a chill grey-blue sky; my forebodings were reinforced.

'Come away,' I said.

'Soon.' And he pulled me nearer the arch, which I saw to be what was left of a porch. Fallen rocks littered the ground. 'See,' Richard said, pointing to a heavy stone that lay half grown over with moss and grass.

At that moment, the moonlight shone so brilliantly that every detail of the scene was outlined. I saw the curling brambles and chest-high thistles quivering in the chill breeze; the marks of chisels made hundreds of years before on the dressed stone; and especially the rough-hewn rock.

Richard stopped and ran his big finger over the weather-worn stone, almost caressingly.

He rose. I saw a puzzled yet intent look on his lean face.

'Odd,' he said. 'I could have sworn — '

I didn't want to hear what he would say. 'Richard, let's get right away from here! This place terrifies me!'

Richard looked down again. 'I've seen that somewhere,' he said.

The evening had been one of the worst I'd known, and I was still woozy from all the alcohol m my bloodstream.

'Can't we go,' I said, near tears.

'Yes. I'm sorry, love — we'll go back now. You weren't serious about moving out tonight?'

He'd heard me. Good.

'I was, but I'll settle for the South tower, Richard Just so long as we get away from this creepy hole.'

'You're tired,' he said, smiling at me like the man I thought I knew. He took my arm and we turned our backs on the chapel. 'It didn't worry me,' he said. 'The curious thing was I thought I'd been there before, and seen something like that head.'

'Well, don't go again,' I ordered. 'I don't like you in this mood — you went into a trance over that rock. I think Jensen and that woman told us about the chapel just so we would come out here and get scared — they're a devious set of bastards, Richard.'

He laughed. I thought of something else. 'What head?'

He looked back into the ravine. Before us was the huge black mass of rocks and Monteine Castle. I looked away as the waves crashed far below us.

'Head?' he said. 'Oh yes. It was almost worn away. You'd need a torch to see it properly. I thought it was a boar's head at first. But it wasn't. It isn't any of the usual heraldic animals. And yet I'm sure I've seen it somewhere.'

I stumbled.

'Rest for a minute or two,' Richard said. He held me for a moment. I sensed a tension in him that had nothing to do with me. I hated the harsh moonlight and the half-buried stone head, with its hint of evil. Richard was staring out to sea, quite unaware of my distress.

'You can't have seen it before,' I said.

He had his whole attention on the streaming glittering moonlight far below us, where the waves rolled black and silver in the unending rhythm of the sea. He made some sort of answering noise, his breathing fast and shallow.

I followed his interest stare, way out beyond the white of the breakers, to the darkness beyond. 'I thought — ' he said, and then I shook him.

'Richard, I've had enough of it all! I don't want to hear about ruins and corpses talking and dead sailors!'

He patted me gently. 'I'm sorry, my love,' he said, and I was back with him now, and he with me. 'I thought a blow of fresh air would be just the thing for ns.'

'Well, it wasn't,' I snapped. 'And I still think those bastards at the Castle wanted to frighten me.'

Richard helped me over a patch of broken rocks.

'Don't let them worry you, Anne. Bed right away?'

It was my turn to stop.

'What were you staring at?' I asked abruptly. 'Just now. Out to sea. You were looking for something.'

'It was a long way out,' he answered evasively.

'There's a lot of seals about this coast.'

He led me on. 'I expect that's it.'

I looked at him, then my attention was caught by a movement high above us, a momentary yet solid movement on the North tower.

'You're ice-cold,' said Richard. 'Let's get back.'

As I was half-supported back to Monteine Castle, I imagined we would slip into the entrance hall and sneak upstairs without being seen; and then there would be the tenderness and release I so desperately wished for.

It didn't happen like that.

The three of them were waiting, huge smiles on their faces and full of badinage about our adventure. They drew Richard into conversation and into an analysis of his strange encounter with the dead fisher crew; and I listened with growing anger, for I refused to say a word to any of them, Richard included

And that was a part of their cunning, for when they began to hint at a legend that centred on the cliffs and the Castle I was icily rude to everyone.

I went upstairs alone, cold and miserable, my thoughts in a kaleidoscopic whirl of moonlight, sea, stones, dead men, clever talk and Richard's cruel smile.

I was half asleep when he came to me, hours later.

He didn't say a word. I thought he was angry, and I prepared to be reluctant; but it was only to be a token show, for I needed him desperately.

He had never been so violent in lovemaking before. He left me with a deep sense of fear. I lay awake, and slept only as the last of night filtered away.

I awoke with a crashing bang, and for a moment I thought Richard had struck me; before that night the idea would have been inconceivable.

In the half-light, I could see Richard sleeping on his stomach, with the bedclothes flung back. His skin glowed. I stretched my hand out and he stirred and smiled in his sleep.

I ran my hand along his spine, hoping he would wake and hold me.

'Richard?' I whispered, moving closer. Then I stroked again, for a curious sensation was transmitted by the nerve-endings of my fingertips.

Richard's skin seemed silkier, I brushed again, puzzled. I looked down.

I could see clearer now, though belief was not yet there. But I had to believe it, for the ridged darkness along the vertebrae was unmistakable. A thick line of black fur ran along Richard's spine.

6

Why, when I felt such horror, I did not scream I do not know. I can only suppose that the submerged and unknown self-protective mechanisms took over.

'No!' I whispered, not knowing what I was denying, but full of a sickening horror.

Richard stirred in his waking sleep and murmured something to me. He knew I was with him, for his arm came out seeking warmth and when he did not find me next to him, he murmured again, puzzled.

Again acting instinctively, I pulled my robe around me as I stood shuddering in the grey of the dawn. I wanted Richard to wake up; but as soon as I thought of touching him again desperately wished him to sleep on, so that he would not see me in this fearful trembling state.

I heard the dull booming of a ship out at sea, then the screaming of gulls about the tower; the room seemed less cold as the grey shadows of the dawn dispersed. The movement of a gull's wings caught my eye and I looked out of the window. Thick, heavy fog blanketed the landscape. The sea was gone, the cliffs were hidden; there was nothing but the heavy grey-white fog. I felt that the entire world consisted of myself, the tower room and the stranger on the bed.

There was a malevolence at the Castle which I could feel as if it were an icy casing about my body.

Minutes passed like that. Gradually, Richard's sleep became lighter. I could hear him stirring. I couldn't look directly at his back, not again.

Quite suddenly, so quickly I was totally unprepared for it, Richard turned smoothly onto his back and sat up.

'Anne?'

He looked tired. There was a pallor under his brown skin, but otherwise he looked like the man I loved. Eyes brilliantly blue, the high cheekbones the same, the hair that especial white-blond of the outdoorsman; and the smoothly muscled body was no different.

'Bad head?' he asked.

'No!'

'I'll order tea. What is the time, by the way?'

He looked as though he might move towards me, and I panicked.

'I'll order the tea! Richard, don't bother — anyway, it's hardly dawn — the sun's just up — '

'Do the staff good. Keep them on their toes,' Richard said heartily. 'I can't have you weak and wan, my love. How about breakfast up here?'

An impossible scene flashed into my head, with Richard saying '*What!*' in an astonished, quizzical way, as I said that I'd seen and felt the hair on his spine and then leaping towards me, full of glee and I would have to hold him and feel the eerie silky fur again, feel it and know it was there, a part of him. The conventions saved me. I remembered that I didn't want the Sievel woman to know we were sleeping together.

'They'll know we're together!'

It was all I could think of.

'Anne, be your age, darling,' he ordered, and then he turned to the phone and I had to look at his back.

My astonishment made me gasp. Richard's spine was clear.

I gave an audible gasp. 'You are jumpy,' he said. 'You'd better get back into bed.'

The black line, the silky black line was gone. I couldn't quite accept it for a moment, and I stood still with an expression of incomprehension on my face. Richard took it for one of aloofness.

'If you're going to play hard to get, Madam,' he said, leaping to his feet, 'then I'm the one to catch you.'

Richard's warm, muscular body was against my cold skin. I clung to him, shaking with tears and laughter.

'You'll never credit for a moment what I imagined!' I gasped. We were under the bedclothes by then. 'Just for a moment, I thought you'd grown a line of black — '

I couldn't say that it was a line of silky fur,

'Grown what?' Richard said.

'I saw a shadow on your back. It was like hair.'

'The things you dream up,' he said. 'Wait!' he yelled as a knock came at the door. 'Leave it outside, please!'

A woman's voice said, 'Certainly, sir,' in the kind of tone that suggests considerable speculative interest.

I didn't have to leave until about ten-thirty; Richard knew it. We let the tea cool, and wouldn't say any more about my imaginings. We both slept, very content and loving, for another couple of hours.

Breakfast was superb. Richard had ordered it before I was awake, so the first I knew of it was the smell of bacon as he took the lid off a platter and let the delicious smells drift before me. We didn't say much. Richard had apparently forgotten my silliness.

After showering together, we both looked well. Richard glowed with health, and I saw that I needed only a little make-up to disguise the fact that I had slept for only about four hours in the past twenty-four.

'You look nice,' Richard told me. 'I'm going to miss you.'

'But surely you'll be coming back to London now?'

Richard grinned. 'I didn't tell you what happened last night.'

'You've got the job?' I said, unsure of my feelings about it.

'The report is entirely favourable just as Jensen said. So you arrived at the right moment, Anne. The only snag is that I have to hang on here to meet International's Chairman.'

'Here, not in London?'

'He likes to come out here. He's a bit of a recluse — Italian, so I've heard. There's a small private airfield about a dozen miles away, and he flies here direct from Venice.'

'And how long will it be before you're back?'

'They aren't sure. I suppose we'll have to consider the details of the contract, and the scope of the job, that sort of thing. Apparently the Chairman has some kind of wasting disease, and he's allowed a trip in a jet only about once every three months. My appointment — the job they're offering me — fits in with his next visit. It could be any day, so they want me on hand. It isn't unreasonable, really. Now, why don't you cheer up and get a dress on? You know you could stay here for the weekend Anne. How about cancelling your appointments?'

'I do have a job to hold down, and I said I'd be back to see Tony on Saturday. But I wouldn't want to stay here if I could — I don't trust them, Richard!'

'You could tell Tony about the job, Anne. It's all right to do that now.'

He was sidetracking me, an old technique. I fell for it because I couldn't help it;

'I'm damned if I'm going to pretend he isn't my son. Not for anyone, Richard — I don't care who knows it.'

'I didn't say — '

'You don't have to stay with me!' I burst out. 'I can go on my way now and I can forget you and all the rest of this.'

'You can't,' he said. Richard knew, of course. 'Don't cry.'

As Richard held me, the last of my fears about Monteine Castle drained away. He always affected me in that way:

some people have the gift of creating a sense of security; I had the good fortune to fall in love with one such.

I don't think I shall ever regain the unthinking happiness we had during those first months together, not ever, not the careless delight.

'Listen, Anne,' Richard said, when I was myself again. 'I know you had your doubts about us. I think I know the reason you came here — it was to tell me you'd decided we should part, wasn't it?'

'How did you know?'

'I know you. Certainly I'm aware of enough about the way you feel to understand that you couldn't be alone for a whole year. You've had enough of being alone.'

I desperately wanted to forget the deep, authoritative voice I had heard after I ricked my ankle in the cold dark passage; equally, I needed to believe in the bright future International would provide for us.

All I could think of was blue seas, white buildings and a permanent sense of well-being. Even so, I made one last try to get Richard to understand my reason for apprehension.

'Jensen did say those things, Richard. He and the others thought I would affect you — they were planning it before dinner.'

Richard had enough sensitivity to listen and consider what I had said.

'Then I'll find out what they were about.'

'But they'll know I've told you!'

It seemed of supreme importance that they should not know I had overheard them. Richard hesitated.

'You know, you could be right, Anne. I'm thinking of what you said last night. It may be that the right thing to do is to pack our bags and walk right out. If you're apprehensive about International now, you may hate being associated with the company out in the Bahamas.'

I accomplished the trick of double-think.

The sea and the sands won. I despise myself now for the easy victory of the travel brochures. I was fool enough to believe in a mirage.

'No, Richard. It's just right for you. Anyway, it isn't as if we need see Jensen and the others again. They're based here in England, aren't they?'

'They're hired as advisers when they're needed. They're not permanent employees. And there's no reason why you should meet any of them again.'

'And you'll come to London soon?'

'Try to keep me away.'

Richard and I went down the winding tower stairs in a glow of happiness about the future. Jensen was waiting.

'Richard! Anne! Delightful to see you looking so well! I must say that the sea air has done you both a power of good.'

I looked about for the Sievel woman and Fitch. Jensen understood. 'Alas, Eric and Monica have duties elsewhere this morning. My dear, I've had Andre bring your car to the front door.'

'Thank you,' I said.

'And Richard, may I offer you my congratulations?'

Richard took the long envelope from Jensen's hand. He thanked Jensen and smiled at me. I knew already what the letter would contain.

He read it and passed it to me. It was

brief and formal. Richard was offered a five-year contract with International at a senior level. The offer was firm, generous and unconditional, and the signature was boldly written in a florid style no longer fashionable. The signatory was *Simon Miaolo*. There was no mention of International on the letter heading, simply an elegant inscription *The Palace, Venice*, and the date, 24th July.

'Dated today,' said Richard.

Jensen smiled. 'Sent by e-mail. The signed original will arrive soon by airmail. Mr. Mialo wanted you to receive his offer immediately.' He beamed at me.

I had a few minutes alone with Richard, and then I was driving away through the narrow lanes busily working out the life style we should have. One memory bothered me.

The bar-steward had seen my departure from Monteine Castle, but he had not been looking at me. He had been staring at Richard with a cold calculation that dismayed me. I forced myself to ignore the memory. The future was so bright.

7

I bought a couple of dozen designs in Oldham and slightly less in Chester; I upped the price for the Chester artist. He wasn't a young man, and he had come to design work by an unusual route. He'd taken a course during his last prison sentence and then he'd realized that he was a better artist than car-thief.

By the time I got to London that evening I was exhausted. I rang Tony's aunt in Streatham and asked if Tony needed me that night. He didn't, since he was tired out after a hard day chasing Gloria's zany labrador around Mitcham Common. I arranged to pick him up in the morning, then I wondered about ringing Richard.

I decided against it. It would seem as if I was unsure of him, that I was pursuing him. It was only a few days, I argued. Then the Chairman of International would come and go, and Richard would be back in London.

I made myself work, cleaning the already spotless flat. Finally I had had enough of my own company and rang Freda Langdon who was my friend and also one of my best customers.

'Alone?' she guessed. 'Richard's still away?'

'Just until next week.'

'It can seem ages. I've a few friends in, some you know. Coming?'

Freda was forty-eight, divorced twice, childless, and dark, with a figure a ballerina might envy. She was absolutely straight in her approach to business, but her love life was invariably devious. She needed intrigue as a duck needs rain. It was nearly twelve by the time I got to her flat in Regent Square, but she dismissed my apologies. She waved to the dozen or so people in the large, old-fashioned room; she hadn't changed a thing from the day she had bought the lease and the whole of the furniture and fittings from a genuine upper-class buck of the Edward VII vintage.

I knew two of the women well, and one

man. The rest were complete strangers. Freda introduced me around and sent a tall, strikingly handsome middle-aged man to get me a gin and tonic. 'He's the one,' she murmured, as she gazed at his back.

'Who is he?'

'Establishment,' said Freda. 'He calls himself a civil servant.' I saw the tall man returning. 'He's very blunt about what he does, so he's got to be Security. He pretends that he's an adviser on tropical agronomics, but can you see him paddling about in the paddy fields?'

He had an air of a man who knows his own mind, the quality of certitude that I responded to in Richard.

'How nice to meet you,' he said. 'Freda said you'd be coming — and, as it happens, I know of Richard Ulrome. What's he doing next, the Three Oceans?'

I couldn't help boasting mildly, 'He's to be an adviser for International Marine Oil in the West Indies.'

'You know how to pick them, you really do, Anne,' said Freda.

'Mr. Miaolo, the Chairman, is flying

out to meet him next week.'

Charles Schofield's eyebrows rose slightly. 'I didn't know he left Venice these days,' he said. 'It must be an important appointment,'

I chattered on happily for a while, then went across to talk to a woman I didn't especially like, but who might keep me in touch with the design business when I was in the Bahamas. I didn't wish to give up what was for me as much a hobby as a job.

I went home when the party broke up at about three. Charles Schofield offered me a lift, but I didn't want to be a trouble to him; or to Freda, who was looking more and more amorous as the evening went on. I found a taxi willing to go out to South Kensington and I had determined to think of nothing but the good things to come.

I did wonder why the tall man and Freda had talked about me though, for they had. I'd overheard one phrase in particular from Freda's new acquisition, a phrase I hadn't liked. In the kind of silence that sometimes comes between tracks on the stereo and in the gaps of conversations, I had heard the tall man say, quite clearly: 'Miaolo's one of the most dangerous men in Europe.'

Freda's new friend had poise, true. And, I speculated, in the appropriate circumstances, he would be a useful man to have at one's side. And *Security*? Well, that was correct euphemism for the intelligence community, so that was pretty obviously why he could come out with such a knowledgeable statement about Richard's potential employer with such complete assurance. I felt a certain tremor of discomfort at this hint — well, it was more than a hint, a warning. But I had a strong man with me already, so did I need Freda's admittedly impressive new guy in my life — or Richard's for that matter? Well, as it happened, I assured myself, fortunately no.

I explained it away. Miaolo was in the most cutthroat business of our times, the oil business. From what I knew of the industry, it needed a venomous skill to make the kind of money he had amassed. But Richard had professional skills that

Miaolo needed, and, anyway, Richard was shrewd, capable and determined. Richard was well able to take care of himself, I told myself.

I slept fairly well, apart from my dreams of Monteine. They were insubstantial, shadowy dreams in which I found myself wandering with no clear purpose around the corridors and winding staircases of the Castle. There was a hint of mocking awareness of my plight on someone's part. I didn't know who the watchers were, but they had a place just beyond the edges of my dreams. Not once did I see Richard though. I remembered that when I awoke and it distressed me.

I kept myself busy so I didn't have to think. When I picked Tony up he took the news that he wasn't going sailing well enough, as I thought he would. I didn't mention the prospect of living in the West Indies. His friends from the flat below called for him after lunch, and they all went off to play in the gardens of the square I lived in.

I got worried when Richard hadn't called by ten that evening. Tony was asleep. The flat was too quiet.

I rang Monteine Castle.

Richard wasn't available. I asked for Jensen and learned that he was at a meeting. 'At half-past ten at night?' I asked. It was so, I was assured. 'Then I'll speak to Miss Sievel.'

'I don't think that any of our consultative staff are available just now, Miss Blackwell,' I was told, very politely.

'When will Mr. Ulrome be available — and anyway, what's he so busy with?'

The woman was smoothly reassuring. Mr. Ulrome, she thought, had been invited out for the evening. She could check if it was urgent; she managed to suggest that I was flapping like a wet hen.

She asked if there was a message she could pass on. I wanted to say 'Get him to ring as soon as he's back', but instead I found myself saying, 'I'll ring in the morning.'

'I'm sure you'll be able to contact him then, Miss Blackwell,' the operator said.

I began to wish I had accepted the pills Freda Langdon had offered. She was quite right. The next week was going to be hell.

On Monday morning, I looked ten years older. Tony developed a slight temperature, so I called in our G.P., instead of taking him to school. I asked him to look at my ankle whilst he was there. 'Not too bad,' he diagnosed. 'You've torn a muscle or two. It'll stiffen if you keep off it. Best to walk and suffer. And this young man can stay in bed for a couple of days.'

Tony was too depressed to argue. His eyes were glassy and his skin felt papery. He was too hot, then too cold; and he didn't like bed. Gloria rang at eleven. When she heard he was ill, she said she was on the way. She's fortyish, fairly wealthy, and unmarried. I don't know why. She'd been the only one of her family to help me. We never mentioned Tony's father. I think he'd gone to South Africa to work, but I wasn't sure. Gloria had a couple of dress shops — she was an excellent businesswoman. But Tony always came first.

Gloria took one look at his pale face and said she'd stay for a day or two. She assumed that I had business to attend to and said she'd cope.

Tony was a little tearful as I left, which didn't help my state of mind. I said I'd look in during the late afternoon.

I knew exactly what I had to do. I'd have an excellent excuse for contacting Richard if there was any mail at his flat.

Richard lived in a first-floor flat in a largish mid-Victorian terrace. He'd once said that the lease on the flat was the only thing his father had left him apart from a few shares in Government stocks. The rooms were large, ornate and furnished with massive mahogany pieces and stiff, uncomfortable chairs and settees. There was an air of impermanence about the place: I didn't much like it although we'd had some pleasant times there. Richard hadn't mentioned picking up his mail. It was my own idea.

I saw a couple of obvious circulars, a message from the hall porter to inform Mr. Ulrome that Mrs, Blaxton couldn't get m that week and maybe next week too because of her back; and, thank goodness, an official-looking letter with the name of a London firm of solicitors on the flap: *Meggitt, Drew and Ainsley.*

I felt my gloom lift: I had a good excuse to ring Richard.

I lifted the receiver, meaning to ring Monteine Castle, when I suddenly thought of checking Richard's answer-phone. I noticed that he had several messages. Putting the receiver back on the cradle, I pressed the play button.

The first four messages weren't important, but the fifth had me reaching for pen and paper as it played.

It was an overseas call:

'This is a message for Richard John Stephen Ulrome. Unable to speak to you direct by telephone after many attempts, so we are leaving this message. Consider the news sufficiently important to contact your family solicitors. Regret to inform you of the death of our client the fifteenth Earl of Monteine, Henry Richard Ulrome. Coroner's officer confirms cause of death as accidental drowning. Letter and copies of reports following. Suggest you contact your family solicitors with despatch, Await your instructions regarding the late Earl's estate. Joseph Sellings for J.N.T. Trusts Inc.'

I was puzzled by so many things about the message that I sat down and wrote it all out, by dint of playing it again three times, until I was certain I had it noted down correctly.

The message was important. It was another of those events that would roar through my life, altering everything.

Richard was to give a New York firm of lawyers instructions regarding the estate of a dead nobleman, the fifteenth Earl of Monteine. Richard had the same name, Ulrome. Richard was the heir. It didn't seem in the least unnatural to think of Richard as a nobleman. It was exciting, of course; but he had always seemed aristocratic. There was something that troubled me though, and I didn't know what.

I sat for quite a while looking at the telephone, at the note in my hands, and then at the letter from the London firm of solicitors. Monteine: I hated the name.

I had the strongest urge to delete the message and destroy my note and the letter.

Would such an action have altered the

course of events?

I knew with a sudden clarity that events were being manipulated by talented men and women who would let nothing stand between them and the accomplishment of their desires.

And yet I could face the unknown evil.

'Mr. Richard Ulrome,' I told the telephone operator at Monteine Castle. 'Yes, it is important.'

8

He hadn't wanted me at Monteine Castle. I drove North full of anger, dismay and apprehension. It wasn't at all like the time before, for then I had been in a dreamy state in which I was playing at telling Richard we were through. This was entirely different, for then I had been certain that he wanted me.

Richard had been hardly coherent over the phone. It had taken several minutes before he could be located, and even then the operator asked me if the call was urgent. I had been astringently icy with her and felt much better for it, but a rising sense of panic kept my gaze riveted on the neat black lettering of the envelope. I was certain what it would contain; he *had* to be glad to get the letter. I was wrong in that, as in so much more.

When he answered he slurred his words. I asked him if he felt well in the tone of voice that meant had he been drinking; he responded with a curt question of his own. What did I want? He was drunk, almost offensively drunk.

As I heard the voice of the man I respected so much demanding to know what I wanted, I had difficulty in holding my temper back. I was ringing him because I feared for him, and for myself, but far more for him. I wanted to explain that Jensen and Fitch and the Sievel woman were scheming against him, and so was the enigmatic bar-steward, whose obsequious manner hid a granite power. I wanted to yell that he should leave Monteine Castle without a second's delay, and that the Italian he was to meet was reputed to be one of the most dangerous men m Europe. I said none of these things.

Already I was revising my judgment of my friend's new guy. Charles Schofield's words had taken root. A mandrake was growing in my mind,

My thoughts cleared in the moment or two whilst he breathed into the mouth-piece of the phone two hundred and fifty miles from me that seemed more like a universe away now. I told him that I had an urgent message for him.

'How urgent?' he asked, when I had penetrated his cold reserve and made him answer with some degree of politeness.

'So urgent I'm on my way with it. And a letter from a firm of solicitors.'

'On your way!' He sounded baffled, and dismayed too.

'Yes.' Before he could say any more, I told him in that I thought he was now a nobleman and that I wanted to be the first to congratulate him. I also said I wasn't far away, another lie. I didn't let him get in a word before I rang off.

Then I rang through to Gloria, to learn that Tony was chirpy if rather ill. He'd had antibiotics and was responding. I went back to the little car and set it howling towards Yorkshire once more. I didn't realize I was touching ninety until a police car flashed me. I stopped reluctantly.

'Have you left a cake in the oven?' demanded a dour and podgy sergeant in a heavy Yorkshire accent. 'We can always get a neighbour to turn the oven off. Little things like that come our way every day.' He noticed my white face. 'Is there something wrong, Miss?'

'I've had some bad news. I suppose I was going too fast.'

He wasn't ironical after that.

'Trouble always keeps. No need to run to it.' He asked if he could help. His co-driver looked at my licence. I didn't want an endorsement, so I thanked him. He was, after all, calming a semi-hysterical woman who was a danger to the travelling public. 'Go easy? Please, Miss?'

'I will, Sergeant.'

He and his co-driver watched me go. I wondered what they made of the encounter for a while, then I decided they did that sort of thing day in day out and they would forget me in an hour.

The big sergeant's calm solidity had made me begin to think again, but I began to feel afraid as soon as I turned for the coast road. I realized that the cold, metallic sensation filling me was the same as that I had experienced in the pre-dawn greyness of the tower room. I thought again of the trick of light and the feel of hair on Richard's cool back.

It was near dusk, about ten o'clock as I drove through Monteine Landing. My thoughts turned to New York. The fifteenth Earl had died m New York. I drove on up the steep cliff road thinking of death in a strange city.

The Castle seemed almost adrift in the thin sea-fret. It loomed huge and grey-white and unreal. I thought of the crudely-carven head, fallen from the arch of the mined chapel. And Richard, with that cold, cruel smile in the harsh moonlight. I had to force myself to go on. I felt furious with Richard for getting so drunk. I was defending him and protecting him from people who were his enemies, and he had rejected me.

I was so annoyed that I stopped the car. I looked up at the massive rock and the castellated towers. There were no lights in the tower where we had slept. The mist from the sea rolled over the high black mound blotting it out, but I could still see lights through the whiteness. I cut the engine of the Fiat and got out. I don't know why. Perhaps I was responding to some primitive instinct when I made the decision to approach Monteine Castle unseen.

I limped the few hundred yards to the great ornamental gates, keeping to the shadowed side of the road. Enough moonlight penetrated the mist for me to see the edge of the footpath. I kept in the deeper shadows. I almost cried out when a great white owl dipped from behind a hedge with only the faintest whisper of sound. I ran for a few steps, then I calmed down.

Far away I heard the lowing of a foghorn, though whether from a ship at sea or from a cliff-top coastguard station I couldn't begin to guess. I felt in a curious state, somewhere between terror and elation.

It was like taking drugs for the first time: as if another person existed side by side with the real me; someone or something watching and daring me on, but not the real me, not Anne Blackwell.

The gates were open.

I had a story ready as I entered the grounds. The engine of the Fiat had cut out. No one could check the story since I had the only set of keys with me. I kept off the path. I could see lights behind the dull red curtains of the ground floor room. I felt inside my coat pocket for the letter and the note.

There had to be a reasonable excuse for my presence. I hadn't taken the precaution of arranging my story in advance with any conscious intent. My knees quivered, and I felt my breath jerking out in short gusts. I was sure I could be seen, even though I was in the gloom of enormous clumps of rhododendron bushes, and the mist was thicker there.

Abruptly the doors opened and a shaft of light suddenly split the mist as a figure emerged. I started to say that the car was down the road, but only a whispered croaking came out. The mist swirled thicker, and the figure was hidden. I knew someone was coming towards me, but all I could hear was a thin sighing of the wind in the bushes, and the regular patter of water dripping from the dark leaves above and around me, 'I've been an idiot,' I managed to say. 'I can't think why I stalled the car. Would you mind trying to start — '

But there were no footsteps. However hard I concentrated, I could hear nothing but the night noises. I began to doubt what I had seen; but the massive oaken doors stood open, and a white beam of light broke solidly through the sea-fret.

I had seen a figure emerge — that of a man. Could it have been Richard? Had he sensed my presence — that I would be reluctant to take the final few steps to the Castle?

But he had been curt, almost surly with me. As I hesitated, I heard voices through the cold, salt mist.

' — shouldn't someone watch?' came the clear voice of the Sievel woman. 'The mist is thickening.'

'No,' said Jensen. I was perhaps twenty yards from them, yet every word carried to me clearly; the sounds seemed to hang in the mist, Jensen's bulk was outlined briefly as the mist swirled, then the damp whiteness swallowed him again. 'The track's so well defined we needn't worry about losing him,' he said.

'I thought it would be useful to observe his actions. Perhaps for the future?' I heard Monica Sievel suggest.

'No,' said Jensen definitely. 'Kresak's instructions must be followed exactly. I think he's right to regard the failure of the Haiti affair as attributable to the presence of sceptics. If there is to be the rapport Kresak expects then Ulrome has to make the initial moves. Exactly what he'll do we can't say — it's difficult to adjust the dosage to his level of — '

Someone interrupted. I didn't hear much, just a dull confusion of masculine voices muffled by the fog from the sea. But I thought I heard my name mentioned. *The Blackwell woman*. Me. Then I heard Fitch's voice, but I caught only the word 'chapel'.

It brought me face to face with the reality of the situation. I knew that Richard was heading towards the chapel.

Why he was doing so was beyond my present state of knowledge. But I had to follow him: there was nothing else I could have done. When they stopped talking and the doors closed, I knew that Richard had gone to the chapel: I had to go to him.

The cliff-top walk was not as dangerous as I might have supposed. The mist was thick but there was a pattern to its dank immensity. For minutes at a time, the banks of heavy sea-fret would shift landwards and engulf the cliffs high above the sea; and then there would be short periods of a few seconds when the path wound before me for fifty yards like a grey-white ribbon. I watched for the line of white limestone beneath the dandelions, thistles and the white flowers of the brambles. I hated Jensen and the others more and more as the thorns lacerated my flesh.

Bravado kept me going despite my hurt ankle. Now that I was at the dark ravine, I had the feeling that more danger lay behind me than any at the chapel

Then I saw the light. I stopped, for there was an altogether different look about the ruins. I moved closer. I could see clearly what had happened. The brick wall had been smashed down; the light came from inside.

The chapel extended into the rock of the ravine for as far as I could see. Richard was inside. Huge shadows hid him from me.

I took a few steps forward.

Richard's back was to me; in his right hand, held high was an oil-burning lantern. Its light was sufficient to illuminate most of the interior, though some parts were in dark shadow. A tightness about my chest and throat kept my prepared questions from being voiced.

Richard was in a trance, his whole being centred on a stone structure before him. There were others. And ranged row on row along the sides of the cavern were cupboard-like recesses. I couldn't speak. My throat muscles were paralyzed. The yellow light wavered as Richard's hand trembled with the effort of holding the lantern close to the slab of stone.

Quite suddenly Richard turned and I saw his face. It was empty of expression; but the lips were tight-drawn and his eyes were slits. He looked as though he could see through the night and beyond any part of the living world.

By then I knew what lay beyond the smashed brick wall: the tombs of the Earls of Monteine. Richard's ancestors.

He passed me without a glimmer of recognition.

I should have screamed if he had touched me.

9

I was still shuddering an hour later when I drew up in front of the Castle. The engine of the Fiat grumbled on for a moment or two and the gravel settled beneath the tyres. There wasn't a sound in the night.

It had taken half-an-hour for my courage to return. I had to face Richard. I stood looking up at the mist-shrouded walls trying to assemble the few facts I knew for certain. My journey back from the chapel had almost exhausted me, what with the steep climb on my wrenched ankle and the absolute need for silence. I had to be calm, for Richard's sake. They were using him, I told myself.

I found a bell push and stabbed at it. The heavy doors swung open and a flood of light illuminated both me and my car.

The dapper little waiter, Andre, recognized me at once:

'Ah, Madam, so you are here at last!

May I take your case? Miss Sievel is expecting you — please, Madam, the keys for the car are in the ignition?'

I let him usher me into the hallway. I looked about me, glad to be out of the dank coldness, but tense too. Monica Sievel walked towards me:

'How nice to see you again so soon, Anne! Richard said you were coming — but you look frozen! How about warming up in the bar before anything else?'

I was so cold. 'Where's Richard?' I asked, without any attempt at politeness. I wanted him out of Monteine Castle, fast. I was afraid for him; and afraid of him too.

'I expect he's in his room or reading in the library. Do try to get warm. What a night it is, Anne! The Yellow Room for Miss Blackwell,' she told Andre. 'Find Mr. Ulrome,' she added. 'Tell him Miss Blackwell has arrived.' Andre hurried away as she guided me to the bar. I was to stay over, she insisted. I watched her eyes. *Did she know?*

I caught an exchange of glances

between her and Max, the bar-steward. In them I thought I read a question; and a reassuring answer. They would not prevent my seeing Richard. The Sievel woman enveloped me with her charm. And Max was equally concerned.

'Can I get you something to eat, Madam?' he asked. *You're Kresak*, I thought suddenly. He had to be.

'What a good thought, Max,' said Monica Sievel. 'Get some soup and sandwiches, will you? But first some whisky. With hot water.'

Jensen joined us. 'We were expecting you earlier,' Jensen said. 'We held dinner over for an hour,'

They were as kindly as cobras.

'I think I should see Richard now,' I said. I swallowed some of the powerful hot brew. 'He sounded quite ill when I rang. How is he?' I made an effort to preserve appearances, though at considerable cost. I had failed Richard at the ruined chapel, for I had turned away from him in silent horror when I saw the frozen and cruel expression on his face I had been terrified of him, and that was a betrayal of the love that we shared. Terrified, I had staggered and reeled away. I had watched him walk away and it was many minutes before I could follow.

Did terror still linger in my eyes, I wondered, as the Sievel woman made reassuring noises to me. Did Jensen's half-smile of concern have as the other half an amused contempt for my ineptness as a liar? Was the bar-steward even now estimating the extent of my knowledge (such as it was) with the thought that the cliffs were high and the sea-fret a constant danger to the unwary?

I saw again the sickeningly abrupt ending to the cliffs. I closed my eyes but there was no comfort to be had, for I recalled the sensation of the black fur on Richard's spine.

Just then, Andre returned to say he thought Richard was in his room asleep. Should he wake him?

'No,' I said. 'He didn't sound well. It's better if he sleeps.'

'I'm sure you're right,' said Jensen.

'Why don't we send your soup upstairs?' said the Sievel woman, 'Anne, you look absolutely all in. Your clothes are damp too. And your shoes.' It didn't rain inside little Italian cars, I thought. Of course my shoes were wet. And my woollen coat. They were soaked by rain and thick wet grass. I didn't offer any explanation; the less one said in an indefensible situation, the better.

'It's all right,' I told her as she accompanied me up the iron staircase. 'I know the way. I didn't mean to ask for a bed. It's just that some important news came up and I thought it better to bring the letter and message personally to Richard.'

'You don't have to explain, my dear. This way,' she said, as I hesitated before the odd-shaped door, the one I had once passed through by mistake. I turned away from it.

'I can find my way now, thanks,' I said. 'Good night.'

Again I had the feeling that all of them were playing an extended game with me; I was sure once more that they had watched me limp along the cliff path, There were such things as infrared glasses for night observation. I'd seen pictures taken through them.

I found myself in the tower, outside Richard's room. I put my hand to the door, wondering whether to knock, then I felt annoyed with myself. Knock at Richard's door?

'Richard!' I said sharply. 'It's me!'

I pushed open the door before he could get out an answer.

My impetus carried me into the room, but I was dreading what I might find. Images stirred across my mind; I saw the high cheekbones white with strain in the light of the oil lamp; I saw his intent gaze on the grotesquely carven stone head; and then I thought of him, so alone and desolate, as he disappeared into the sea-fret.

A single green shaded light illuminated the room, the twin of the Yellow Room, but here the colour-scheme was green.

He was asleep in a chair, looking thin and drawn. I crossed to him. He was breathing in a shallow, rapid way that I recognized.

Richard was not drunk. He was

drugged. I know the effects of drugs.

'What have they done to you, my darling?' I whispered.

He hadn't moved, except for the shallow rise and fall of his wide, deep chest, His hands were almost translucent in the shadowy light over the dressing table.

I stood quite still for a few moments.

There was a coldness about the air that made my skin creep. An unnatural green dimness hid more than was revealed by the single dark-green shade of the light above the dressing table. Richard was a part of the green darkness. I rubbed my eyes. The light was growing fainter, the shadows deeper. My fingertips tingled, I didn't dare to speak. I knew the hateful grip of terror once more.

I knew that something evil was m the room. I could almost smell it, dank, with the foetid stench of long-dead things cast up by the sea.

I don't know what made me look into the far corner by the window, where an ornate, gilded mirror filled a small recess. It could have been a trick of light and shadow, something horrific or nothing at all, that made me look in the mirror. I looked, and all my strength and resolve sank away in a second. It was like diving into clear water and finding yourself in freezing darkness. I looked in the mirror. It sounds simple enough. And I saw the chair where Richard was sitting, reflected in the mirror.

A high-backed leather armchair with deep wings. But, in the chair, nothing!

I looked harder. I had to, for the room seemed to be filling with a swirling darkness. The stench of rotting things hung thickly. My hands and face broke out in a chilling perspiration. I could almost feel the dank tendrils of dark-green mist on my skin.

There had been nothing in the chair. But now I saw something, not a bodily shape at all,

Terrified, I watched a shape emerge in the grim swirling darkness. It was evil, monstrous, beyond all reason.

Where Richard should be sitting, there was a frightful shadowy *something*.

I looked for a full minute or more at

the swirling green greyness surrounding the chair.

I had to turn, otherwise I should have gone out of my mind.

I had already deceived myself about the dark line on Richard's back, and I was prepared to convince myself that Richard's interest in the chapel had been promoted as some kind of psychological experiment or test by the International staff: macabre, but with a rational explanation. This was different.

I turned away, but I couldn't close my eyes. The after-image of the scene in the mirror stayed with me. I blinked and found myself forced to look at Richard.

Blessedly, the grotesque evil shape was gone. Richard was still himself; no swirling green-grey horror hung over the chair.

I cried out in relief.

I wished at that moment that I had a faith. There was a need for some words of ritual, or a symbolic action: a prayer, the clasping of hands. I said the words but they meant nothing. I had for too many years trusted only in my own self-sufficiency.

'Richard?' I said aloud. He was still in

some kind of coma. But he was Richard. And the fearful shape that seemed to envelop him was gone. I looked in the mirror again.

And saw only a chair and a sleeping man.

I couldn't allow myself to ask what I had seen. I was determined that I would not begin to explore the evil at Monteine. I knew it was too powerful for me

'It was a shadow,' I said, knowing that I lied.

Richard stirred. He must have heard me. I looked closer at his face. His colour was back. There was a slight pallor about the skin, but the harsh savage lines on his lower face had gone He murmured something to me, and I felt a sudden flooding of revulsion against all that had happened to him and around him that appalled me. I knew I loved him, but I couldn't feel any warmth at all.

When he opened his eyes, I was sure he couldn't see me properly, just a vague presence.

'Anne?' he said. 'I knew you were here.'

'I'm here,' I said. 'Richard, what's happening?'

I saw his pupils were pinpointed. I'd seen heroin addicts with the same remoteness. I was angry and frightened. Richard had been drugged.

'Anne?' he said again.

I looked at the telephone, but how could I call for help? They were using drugs on him. Hadn't Jensen said I was a druggie? I had to know the symptoms; and if I voiced my opinions they'd know I suspected them. But of what?

I grabbed Richard's cold hand as I heard Andre's voice in the adjoining room, my room.

'Madam? Madam, I have brought your supper! I shall leave it outside the room. Thank you, Madam!'

'Thank you, Andre,' I whispered, as I released Richard's hand. He was watching me.

I stared into his brilliant blue eyes. They were different. The pinpoints had gone but there was a reserve that had not been there before. He looked puzzled but wary too. The effects of the drug were clearing fast.

He looked genuinely pleased to see me,

yet he didn't get out of his chair to take those two steps that should have brought us together.

'I must have dozed off,' he said.

Still he didn't come near me, and I was glad of it.

'Why were you at the chapel tonight?' I asked him briefly.

'I'm sorry, Anne? At the chapel?'

He didn't know he had been out in the dark sea-fret. I felt a suffocating sense of oppression. Richard's face cleared slowly as if he were just awakening.

'It doesn't matter,' I said wearily. 'I'll have to get some sleep.'

'Look, why don't we go into your room?' he suggested.

'No.'

I couldn't have him near me tonight. I wanted to see him in the sunlight before I knew for certain that he was still the man I loved.

I placed the letter and the message note on the dressing table. 'I rang about these,' I said. 'I didn't open the letter.'

Richard got to his feet uncertainly, his face haggard. 'Yes, you rang, didn't you?'

He took the letter and examined the superscription as if he'd never opened an envelope before.

'I have to get some sleep. Good night, Richard,' I said. 'Call me about eight, will you?'

He followed me.

'Of course, my dear. Look, I hope nothing's wrong? It isn't Tony, is it?'

'Maybe I've caught his bug. He isn't too good. Sleep well my love.'

I looked at the tray of now-cold soup, sandwiches and coffee-service. I left them where they were. It was a mockery to send them to me.

I have never been so glad to be able to close a door and blot out the rest of the world.

For a long while I lay awake, listening to the noises of the night, deeply afraid, and very much aware of Richard in the next room.

I was so glad he was not with me.

And yet I loved him with all my heart.

10

I was awake from five o'clock trying to arrange my shattered thoughts. Richard was the centre of it all, and he was obviously in the grip of some memory-obliterating drug.

He had been genuinely puzzled by my enquiry, and then he had appeared to shake free of my questioning. I had to face the bizarre consequence of Richard's answer: he hadn't known he had been at the chapel, and he couldn't bring himself to ask why I should mention it.

This was a classic symptom of a drug-induced state: I knew. I'd seen enough of the effects of addiction.

'Anne?' Richard called at six, knocking softly on the door.

'It's open,' I called back. I'd got up to unlock the door after dawn.

Richard sat on the bed and reached towards me, and for a moment I believed it was all right and then it wasn't, for my hands found his hard-muscled back and I jerked away with something like revulsion.

'Anne, you have got that bug,' he said 'You're ill!'

'I didn't sleep too well.'

Richard knew something was very wrong. 'Tell me, Anne?' he said. 'We don't have secrets.'

I could have wept. I touched him and thought of the line of dark fur-like down then I shuddered, but I couldn't face Richard and say I thought that he was being manoeuvred towards an involvement with a horrifying evil.

I was sure that it would all be over between us if I voiced the least of my suspicions. I thought he would believe me to be a tiresome, neurotic bitch. Better to keep my feeling to myself. That way I should have time to find out the reasons for the dreadful way he was being manipulated. I tried to be calm, as if only mildly curious.

'Why did they talk so much about the supernatural?' I asked.

'You don't mean Eric Fitch's story

about the yodelling cadaver?'

He was mildly amused, nothing more.

'They talked about other things too,' I said. 'All macabre.'

'I'll have a word with Fitch. And Jensen. I can see they had no right to disturb you.'

'Nor you.'

'You're sensitive to atmosphere, Anne. But nothing's wrong here, whatever Fitch and Jensen were hinting at. Every old building has its legends. Why, England wouldn't be the same without its ghosts and ghoulies.'

I hated the flippant way he spoke. This was the man who last night had been entranced by the sight of an ages-old tomb.

'What about the that phone message I gave you?'

Richard looked embarrassed. 'Oh, I knew. They got though to me here.'

'You're an Earl.'

It sounded as though I were accusing him of something.

'Odd kind of development.' He sounded amused. 'I didn't know anything at all about the family connection. My father was always tight about family matters. We're a junior branch of the family, but it seems the line faded out over the past fifty years, so we're the most direct claimants after the fifteenth Earl. It seems he'd settled in New York, poor old devil. But you don't want to hear about my squalid family. I've only just found I'm related to the Monteine breed, love, and I don't give a damn about being an Earl. There's nothing left of the estate but a couple of worked-out mines in Derbyshire and the right to present a sprig of parsley to the Prince of Wales a fortnight before lambing time or something like that.'

New York.

I remembered the deep, authoritative voice, and a cold gripping sensation filled me with renewed fears: there had been mention of a completed New York operation.

I remembered the words: '*It can't be kept from her. We can't arrange another major settlement*'.

'What's the matter?' Richard asked. 'Don't you want to join the ranks of the impoverished aristocracy?'

'You'll be the Earl of Monteine,' I said, thinking of the rows of stone coffins. 'How did he die?'

'Who?'

'The Earl. The one who died in New York.'

Richard shrugged. 'An accident, so the London solicitors say. He was in his seventies, Anne. Why?'

'Nothing!'

'You are getting broody, my love!'

I flinched away from him and he saw it. I hated the hurt look in his eyes, but still I couldn't reach out to him, Suddenly, my mind cleared.

'I think I'll go back to London this morning. I'm a little worried about Tony.'

Richard saw I was determined. I could guess he was thinking that I was oversensitive to atmosphere, and also a bit overwhelmed by the International staff. He went for a shower, looking much happier that I'd decided to leave.

For no particular reason, or perhaps to stop myself thinking, I fiddled with the switches on the bedhead as Richard began to splash. I didn't look especially to see what I was doing; most hotels of a reasonable standard have the usual range of programmes. I didn't like the sound of a local news announcer, and twiddled again.

I was sitting up in bed, and the sight of the television screen glowing into life caught my eye. I didn't switch it off — there would be children's programmes at that time in the morning, I knew that. The features of a sharp-faced elderly man snapped into focus. There was a violence in his ascetic features that drew me forward slightly, and a refined, constrained but deadly quality in his enunciation of English that terrified me. He looked like the Venetians in the library. He had that same look of arrogance and cunning and the words he spoke were like the sound of funeral knells. I can remember what he said, word for word:

' . . . and you will concentrate every effort on the Ulrome enquiry!'

I could see that though he had been a large man he was worn down by age and fanaticism to the point of emaciation. His eyes glared with an overriding and compulsive authority that kept me from calling out in my suddenly terror-stricken state.

What he had to say kept me listening and staring with an ice-cold certainly that I was about to learn the reason for the weird and grotesque things I had seen at Monteine Castle. I knew who he was. There could be no question of it. He was a man who could have ruled an empire — and did in a sense. I was looking at an image of the Venetian, Simon Miaolo, and listening as he arranged the future of Richard.

'Kresak has explained,' he said in that precise, deadly voice. 'Make no mistakes. My patience is unlimited, but my time becomes less. Success is what I promised myself. If there is anything — *anything* — that should be done, name it. You will be failing in your duty if you keep back any circumstance that affects the outcome of the Monteine operation. Remember only this. If for one moment, on one occasion, some proof of the existence of that power or force we seek can be achieved — *once* — however vague however insubstantial, however indefinite: only so much proof as will make the slightest crack in my lifelong agnosticism, then you will have your promised rewards, and I mine! But there will be no excuse for inadequacy and no mercy for incompetence. Kresak has my orders. On this point, be sure.'

I expected the voice to stop and the image to fade; but the picture held firm, and the snapping lips and teeth jerked again in that merciless whiplash of a voice:

'So far, every report I have had suggests careful planning. So far, I am satisfied. But nothing must interfere with the arrangements for the thirty-first! I shall supervise the final details personally. Meanwhile, until the end of the month, be alert and careful! Obey Kresak in all things!'

The image did fade then. I heard the noise of the shower and Richard humming a song to himself. It sounded so normal so ordinary, Then I felt myself go rigid at the memory of that grim face. 'Richard!' I called

'What?'

'See!' I said, as Richard padded into the room leaving wet footprints on the thick pile of the yellow carpet,

Only a nursery rhyme came from the expensive television receiver, and the images were those of a children's presenter.

With a shaking hand I pointed again at the screen. 'It *was* on there. He was talking about Monteine, it was Miaolo, it had to be!'

Richard stopped towelling his hair. 'Anne, what on earth are you talking about?'

'There was a terrible old man. Richard, he's the one who directs Kresak — he's the one who gives the orders!' The old man's eyes had a glittering rage that reached out and through me. I felt he was watching me even now. 'For God's sake, what do they want?' I said more quietly, for Richard looked bewildered.

It was then that I had the thought that the International staff were probably listening in to our rooms. Miaolo would not allow me to interfere with his plans. I knew, with a grim certainty, that I would not be permitted to halt whatever it was they were planning. Miaolo meant what he said.

'Look, Anne, you've been watching what? A talk by someone in the Castle?'

'Yes!'

'They use closed-circuit TV all the time. What did you hear that's turned you broody again?'

'Nothing really.' I looked at the light fitting, at the radiator, at the scrollwork of the dressing table. All that I said would even now be going onto silent, unsleeping tape. 'I expect it was a training film. There was some kind of pep talk from the Chairman.'

'But it scared you. You know, this place isn't doing you any good — '

'I wasn't scared!' I lied, 'It was just that I was expecting that children's programme that's on now. Tony watches it.'

'I think you had better go back to him, Had you better see the doctor too, Anne? You look pale. It's cold on the coast here. Get him to give you a checkup.'

I could have screamed. Richard telling

me to keep my cool when all around him were his enemies. I was losing him, I could see it in his candid gaze.

'Richard, promise me one thing?' I said, 'If you need me, ring right away. Any time.'

'I promise,' he smiled,

Everyone looked quite glad to see me leave. There were no questions by the Monteine Castle staff. No hint that my departure would be impeded. I looked the Sievel woman straight in the eyes and told her that I'd enjoyed my stay; when Eric Fitch congratulated me on my impending elevation to the peerage, I was as graciously bitchy as I could manage, smiling sweetly the whole time; with Jensen I was jokey, and I accepted Andre's help with the luggage. But I couldn't look at the barman, Kresak.

I wanted to get away quickly.

Richard waved at the Fiat until he was lost to sight. I knew what I was going to do by then. People help people, if you can persuade them to do so.

I was going to use every resource I possessed, everyone I knew.

11

Tony was not especially glad to see me. I had a brief moment of dismay when I saw how easily he could adapt to life with his Aunt Gloria; then I saw him grinning at me and forgave him for his suspected disloyalty.

'When's Richard coming back?' he wanted to know. 'John at my school says he hasn't got a boat. He is going to take me to see it, isn't he? Anyway, why don't you marry him?'

Gloria wasn't too happy about the idea. 'Your mummy doesn't want to marry anybody.'

Suddenly I wasn't sure about anything. 'Can he stay for a few more days?' I asked Gloria. 'I've a few things to see to.'

'You've hardly seen the child in a week.'

'No, you haven't,' said Tony, capitalizing on a weakness. 'I'll stay though.'

'How many days?' asked Gloria.

'Until the end of the month.'

'I'll mark it down,' said Tony. He went across to the large kitchen calendar and blocked the date in with a felt-tipped pen. The lettering caught his eye. 'It says someone's birthday, when you come back,' he said.

I looked at the inscription for the first of August. *Lammas Day*. It worried me, but I didn't know why, that there was something about the date I had seen before.

'Be good for Aunt Gloria,' I ordered. Tony looked at me in some amazement.

'I always am!'

'All right, take your medicine.'

'He likes it,' Gloria said with some acerbity, so I stopped fussing and returned to my flat.

It was five in the afternoon, and I wanted some help.

I tried several numbers. The first was a quiet utterly self-possessed middle-aged man I had been friendly with on a casually intimate basis in my mid-twenties for about a year; he was something of a financial wizard, though he lived modestly. He hadn't wanted to part, but he didn't excite me after the first few months, and I was reluctant in those days to join the establishment; and Jimmy Hatton-Stuart was establishment.

'Tell me exactly what is your interest in Simon Miaolo,' he said, from his office. 'No, I'm not busy for ten minutes. Why do you wish to know about Simon Miaolo?'

I was prepared. I couldn't have told him about the moment when I had caught a glimpse of something swirling and evil about the chair where Richard had been sitting, no more than I could have described the absolute revulsion I felt now when I touched. So I told him a part of the truth,

'I'm with Richard Ulrome.' He knew and said so. 'And International Marine Oil are hiring him.' He'd heard a rumour of that too. I was pleased and annoyed that he still followed my involvements. 'Jimmy,' I said, 'I'm serious when I say this: Richard's in some sort of trouble.'

'With Miaolo?'

I drew a breath, for there was a warning in the way he had spoken. 'I think so.

There's a very definite connection between Richard and International's Yorkshire place, Monteine Castle. Did you know that Richard's ancestors owned it?'

He hadn't, there being no reason why he should. I told him that Richard was now the Earl of Monteine.

'That might be important. Tell me, what else is troubling you?'

I left out some of it. I couldn't tell Hatton-Stuart about the weird black fur on Richard's spine, or the swirling thing I had seen in the mirror; but I gave him a fair account of the rest.

'How much does Ulrome mean to you?' he asked, when I had finished.

'Everything.'

He hesitated, and I could almost hear him assessing what he had felt for me against an instinct for self-preservation that had kept him rich when the other city gamblers had toppled in the last crash. 'Miaolo still controls about a fifth of Europe's oil,' he said. 'And an important fifth, But he doesn't care about it.' Again there was a pause.

'So what does he care about?'

'Death.'

'Jimmy — '

'I'm a big fish, my dear,' said the man I had once admired so much. 'But if Miaolo knew I had advised you, I should be swallowed and absolutely digested. Will you take my advice?'

'I don't know.'

'Cut your losses.'

'And come to you?' I said bitterly.

'Only if you wish, my dear. Miaolo is in love with death. Keep away from him. That's all I can do for you.'

He hung up on me.

A charming but bankrupt lawyer was next. He told me how to find out Miaolo's connections with International, then he told me not to bother, since no one doubted Miaolo's control over the group. I refused another invitation and kept on ringing round. Both company directors of multi-nationals I could claim acquaintance with were out of the country. One secretary was inquisitive, the other hostile. I was running out of names by then, for some numbers in my phonebook were used by new subscribers,

Then I rang a sweet and erudite young man called Bill Marr who had helped me look for some Berwick prints a year or two ago; I had used them for headscarves, towels, kitchen utensils; I thought of the innocent country scenes as I waited for him to answer. He still worked in the library.

'Is it Anne Blackwell?'

'Yes, Bill!'

I fended him off as I had before with courtesy and care for his feelings. 'Look, Bill, would you believe it, my future husband — '

I told him about Richard and me with tact and at the same time quiet desperation, for my head was swimming with the effort of concentration. I had driven over two hundred miles in heavy traffic; I hadn't eaten since a sandwich for lunch. I repeated my story: Richard was now an Earl. So I wanted a rundown on the most interesting of the family connections. The Castle. The causes they had supported. Their connections, their women, the outstanding men; and especially, I insisted, their legends.

'Monteine Castle.' said Bill, brightening with the true zeal of the scholar. 'The Ulromes? Yes, I have read something. I'm sure I could dig it out. Is it urgent?'

I said it wasn't, but Bill had got the message. He said he'd ring back in an hour if there was anything on the shelves, otherwise it might take a day or two. But he would do it. I used the last of my charm and let the receiver drop into the rest.

Someone rang almost immediately.

'Richard?' I said automatically.

'No, it's — '

I almost told the caller to get off the phone, but then I realized that it was a friendly voice; and that I had met someone recently who could help me.

'I know. Freda,' I said. I didn't need to use any finesse with her. 'I've got to see your friend,' I told her.

'No chance, darl — '

'It's serious!'

'You do mean Charles Schofield?'

'Yes, Is he there?' Women always know. Somewhat reluctantly, Freda said:

'As a matter of fact, he is. I'll put him

on. You will tell me if I can do anything though?'

I said I would. 'Charles Schofield,' I heard.

I tried to be coherent. I heard myself telling half of what I wanted to tell him, and some of the things I wanted kept secret. Altogether I made such a mess of it that I tried to start again.

'I think I've got the drift,' said the calm, urbane voice. 'First, do you need any help right away? I could get someone to you within five minutes, if necessary.'

'No. It's nothing here.'

He accepted it. 'Good. Stay there.'

'But I wanted you to tell me what I've got to do.'

'All right. Stay there. Wait. Don't take any alcohol or drugs, but eat if you can. Will you do as I ask, Anne?'

'There isn't time to sit about!'

'Twenty, twenty-five minutes, depending on the traffic. I'll bring Freda.'

'No — '

'It's settled then. 'Bye for now.'

I did exactly as Charles Schofield said. I looked in the fridge and found some goulash. Then I sat by the phone waiting for Bill Marr's call, but it didn't come.

When Charles Schofield arrived, there was no hint that he and Freda had just got out of a warm bed. He looked superb: elegant, tanned, not a hair out of place. Freda's eyes were slightly bloodshot; she said she'd make coffee.

'Let her, please,' said Charles Schofield.

'I don't know anyone else,' I said. 'I'm sorry about dragging you into this — '

He silenced me with a gesture. 'You need advice. Have you spoken to anyone else?'

'I told a financier friend about Miaolo. He was scared.'

'Rightly. Go on.'

I explained about my other calls, including the one to Bill Marr. One thing led to another and gradually I told him most of it; but not at all logically or coherently. I left out things; I couldn't bring myself to talk about the sight of Richard in the resting-place of the Earls of Monteine; nor of the dreadful sight in the tower room.

'I heard them talking! This Kresak

— he isn't a bar-steward!'

'Kresak?' said Charles Schofield. There was an added smoothness in his voice.

'You've heard of him?'

'Possibly. How did you meet him?'

I explained, without holding anything back, about my eavesdropping.

'So you believe the bar-steward at Monteine Castle is called Kresak? Describe him, will you, Anne?'

He nodded when I had finished. 'He sounds like Miaolo's troubleshooter. In his case it's an apt title.'

My heart lurched. 'They were talking about a death in New York. Richard was the heir! Don't you see? The man in New York died and Richard became the sixteenth Earl.'

Schofield didn't seem particularly impressed. 'So you think they're setting Richard up for something? You've seen Monteine Castle and its people. What do they want of him?'

'If only I knew! But I saw that awful Miaolo man on the closed-circuit television, and he said Richard had to be ready for something by the thirty-first of this month.'

'And what's the object, do you think? Why has it to be this month?'

'Miaolo was so urgent.' I had it then. 'He looked like a man who knew he might die soon. Someone told me today that Miaolo was in love with death.'

It startled the urbane man sitting before me. 'That's an odd turn of phrase,' he said. He looked towards the kitchen and I saw that the door was firmly closed. Freda had been given her instructions. Schofield was much more than an adviser on new strains of rice. 'A very odd phrase.'

'Why?' I was afraid of the answer. Schofield paused for a while, then he seemed to make up his mind,

'Simon Miaolo has spent the last thirty years in trying to avoid the one inevitability of life. In doing so, it's certain that he has brought death to others.'

'New York? The death of the fifteenth Earl?'

Schofield looked down at his small, capable hands, then he looked up at me, and his eyes were cold. 'Why not find out?'

A link was missing. 'I'm sorry, find out what?'

'Go to New York.'

'But it's thousands of — '

'A few hours on a jet. I'll give you a name at police headquarters.'

'I'm not qualified, I'm just an ordinary person.' But the idea had taken shape. 'It would take at least two days, and besides I'm sure something's going to happen at Monteine Castle.'

'What?'

'I told you. After he'd been to the chapel, I saw a dreadful shape in the mirror. It was evil. And Richard — '

I stopped. I hadn't told him.

'Go on.'

I wished I hadn't started. It sounded ridiculous to me. 'He was at the chapel.'

'The chapel?' prompted Charles Schofield. 'What is the significance of the chapel?'

'I think they're up to some devilry there.'

I expected anything but Charles Schofield's reaction. His calm urbanity disappeared for a few seconds.

'Again you use the right word. Simon Miaolo has had his name connected with devilry before.'

There was pity in Charles Schofield's

eyes. 'God help you both,' he said. 'I wish I could.'

'Richard won't listen to me,' I said. I realized then what Charles Schofield had meant by that pitying look 'You can't leave him! They've got to be stopped!'

'From doing what?'

I told him the rest of it, keeping back nothing this time.

There was a long silence when I had finished.

Freda dropped a piece of crockery into the quietness, probably to remind us that she was supposed to be making coffee and wasn't listening. The sound echoed around the kitchen and reverberated through the still, warm air of the lounge.

'From what you've told me, an international oil company is hiring a young executive on excellent terms. He's waiting to be interviewed by the head of that company — an honour, anyone told that would agree. He's been behaving peculiarly, according to you, but just consider what he's actually done. He's made two known trips, to you, to see a ruined chapel by moonlight, and on one of the occasions he invited you along. A very natural curiosity, at any time, the more so since he learned that the crypt contained the remains of his ancestors.'

'And walking there alone at night? An unusual taste, but not unaccountable, You might add that you've overheard someone saying that he goes there every night — but what's hearsay? And you were eavesdropping, Anne. If anyone in authority were to take evidence from you, what have you to offer but a general feeling of insecurity?'

I felt myself getting angry with him, but his careful and rather anxious look kept me from boiling over. 'Who is to do what?' he went on. 'You are a young woman with an artistic background who is anxious about a young man. He is a famous yachtsman and the heir to an earldom. You'll explain that you think he was under the influence of drugs administered without his knowledge or consent, for reasons you can't put a name to; then you'll be asked how you know about drugs. It will then come out that you once led a slightly irregular life; that you've a medical history of imbalance

— and you'll be patronized, suffered for a while, then dismissed with varying degrees of courtesy.'

'So I am to do nothing?'

'I haven't said that.'

He was still regarding me with that careful, almost calculating expression. I thought suddenly that it was time I paid attention to him, fully, not with half my mind. I was completely in control of myself when he began to explain what I could do.

'Freda!' I called. 'Bring the coffee, please.'

Freda did so, then looked from him to me. 'Well, Anne?'

I didn't know how much to tell her; Charles Schofieid helped me. 'Anne's told me her problem. There's nothing very much I can do directly. She's involved with some extremely vicious people, but they haven't transgressed against any law in this country.'

He let the politeness and the caution slip from his face, and I saw the pity again. 'Anne has no one to rely on but herself.'

Freda defended me by saying with some heat:

'But you're some sort of secret service

official aren't you?'

Charles Schofield smiled tiredly. 'Isn't that the point Freda, my dear?'

'Oh,' Freda said, after a few seconds. I had got the point quicker.

'Charles knows people,' I said. 'He's doing as much as he can for me.'

Freda was very interested, but still a little hurt by his apparent refusal to become involved directly. 'I hope he is!'

Charles Schofield drank his coffee appreciatively, then took out a diary and scribbled for a few moments, He tore off the page and passed it to me. There were two names, one with an address in Norfolk; the other had only a long telephone number. 'This man you should mention my name to,' Schofield said. He didn't say the name aloud. It was the one with the telephone number: *Lieutenant John de Vito*, I read. 'A New York number,' he explained when he saw my puzzlement. 'The other man doesn't know me but he'll be expecting you.'

There was just a surname: Ruane. And an address: *St. Adelburgh's, Monk Alston, Norwich*.

'Don't be misled by appearances in either case, Anne,' Charles Schofield warned me. 'Both of these men are most unusual, and both are experts in their own particular line. Now, how else can I help you?'

'I'm more grateful than I can tell you, Charles,' I said. 'And to you, Freda. Without you, I'd have gone over the edge and tried something ridiculous, like going to Monteine Castle and burning it to the ground.'

'I can't imagine you being violent,' said Freda in some agitation. 'That sort of thing can't help!'

Charles Schofield met my gaze. I recognized now that there was a considerable potential for direct action in him too; I had the feeling that he knew all about violence.

'Try the experts first,' he said.

Freda looked bewildered. If I hadn't felt so excited and tired and eager to be done with the swirling evil that encompassed Richard, I might have been amused at her efforts to contain her curiosity. Charles Schofield was quite the best she had met since I had known her.

I can make decisions quickly. I have to. It can make clients wary, and sometimes my artist and designer connections positively hostile; but I like to know what I'm involved in, and I find it better to ask the right questions if I'm in any doubt about a deal or a venture. I had such doubts.

'I am grateful, Charles,' I said. 'Truly. I can see that a New York detective is absolutely the right source — I've no concerns there. But this Ruane person. In what field does his expertise lie? I mean, what is his line of work?'

Schofield's handsome face suddenly became grim.

The jaw tightened and the dark blue eyes seemed full of a dire knowledge.

'Work? You will judge for yourself, Anne, when you meet him. And please don't be hasty to come to a judgment. Ruane is not what he will seem to be, at first meeting. As for his work, you will have to use your natural intelligence, which is considerable — and your intuition — to be able to make a reliable estimate of his abilities. All I can say at this time is that his work is not of this world. Try to trust him, Anne. If you can.'

That wasn't all, though.

Charles murmured something, for himself, I assumed, not for my ears. And certainly not for Freda's. I caught a quietly and almost inaudible phrase as he smiled reassuringly.

Did I get it right?

It was a Latin tag I'd heard before. I couldn't place it, and I might well have misheard it completely. *Opus Dei*, was it? Probably.

God's work?

The metaphysical implications didn't do much to calm my fearful speculations: what I needed was something tangible to hold on to. A tough New York cop sounded about right. I had to settle for the enigmatic Ruane, however: for now.

Charles held my hand for a moment.

'I'll book the first New York flight tomorrow. But I'll go down to Norwich tonight,' I said.

Freda began to say something until Charles Schofield pressed her arm slightly. 'I've always found it better to move fast,' he said. 'Anyway, you wouldn't sleep.'

'No,' I said. I didn't want the dreams to come back. 'I'll eat something and go right away.'

'That's right,' said Charles Schofield. 'You need your strength.'

12

Charles Scbofield had suggested that I could pick up a visitors' visa at the American Embassy next day — he told me how it could be arranged — and I could be in New York within a few hours. A Transworld mid-afternoon flight was the first one available; it would get me to Kennedy Airport at five-thirty local time. I booked the night-flight back to Heathrow, allowing myself some eight hours to see John de Vito. It would have to be enough time.

The effort of making a decision had helped. Schofield had been right: it was altogether better to rely on oneself, and, full of a quite real sense of hopeful determination, I had set out for the Fens. I would persuade the unknown Ruane to give me what help he could, and then make a rapid visit to the New York policeman de Vito.

Monk Alston is a cluster of thatched

houses and a redbrick pub huddled around a large duck-pond; the most prominent of its features is a thirteenth-century church on a small hill half a mile from the centre. I reached the village by a roundabout route, since that's the way the roads are in the Fen country.

The day was pleasant, warm and with enough cloud cover to make driving easy as I drove across the wide sweeps of flat farmland. It looked so pleasant. They'd started with the harvest, there was a gold warmth across the fields; there wasn't a hint of the grimness I shall always associate with the North-East coast of England. Monteine Castle was a part of a different world.

It was about ten when I reached Monk Alston. I stopped by the pub, where a few teenage boys were trying to ingratiate themselves with a pair of girls about their own age; they were all glad of a diversion. I was the stranger, unifying their little gathering. 'Is that church St. Adelburgh's, please?' I asked.

Two of the boys guffawed, and the girls laughed at my dismay.

'Naoww!!' one of the boys said. 'That's the place where they have the — '

He couldn't finish for laughing, and I felt that familiar apprehension that had been so much a part of my life in the past few days. Charles Schofield had given me something to hope for.

But the boy's inane laughter was to shatter my composure. His contempt for St. Adelburgh's indicated that I must cease hoping.

'Can I help?' asked a middle-aged woman.

She had come out and watched, and I had been almost unaware of her. She was thin and small, well-dressed in a careless sort of way as if she had once liked clothes very much but now considered dress-sense irrelevant. 'You mentioned St. Adelburgh's, I think?'

'Yes, I am looking for St. Adelburgh's. I've just come from London.'

'It's about a mile along the Bixtry road,' the woman said. I looked at her and saw thin, strong features and dark, sad eyes. 'I could show you, if you wish.'

'I don't want to take you out of your

way,' I said, for she was offering to accompany me in the car.

'It isn't out of my way,' she said. 'I work there.'

I didn't want her to say any more. I had been sure the mellow church was St. Adelburgh's and that Ruane was the incumbent, or some sort of scholar who was associated with the church. I had built my expectation on a projection of a distinguished-looking and erudite man who would tell me exactly what kind of devilry Miaolo intended for Richard; and exactly how to circumvent it.

I began to worry, for we were not driving towards the church. For one thing, the woman hadn't asked why I wanted St. Adelburgh's and I wondered why not.

We motored on through narrow lanes for a few minutes.

'Here we are,' said the woman.

We had stopped outside a semi-circular drive, which led to a largish early nineteenth-century brick-built mansion, somewhat battered and neglected looking. It was quite alone in a couple of acres of gardens. I could see unreclaimed land about half a mile away. There were extensive flowerbeds though they had a half-abandoned look about them. A tennis court's rusting wire sagged over part of the drive.

The woman looked at me. It was up to me to speak.

'Thanks,' I said. 'I've come from London to see someone. This is St. Adelburgh's?'

Night had come, and fast. There was no notice board of any kind.

'It is,' she said, and got out of the car. Before she closed the doors, she added: 'Have you someone here?'

'No!'

'All right,' she said. There was compassion in her eyes. 'I hope you find what you're looking for.'

I got out of the car and followed her.

'Wait, please,' I said. She waited. 'What is this place?'

'Don't you know?'

'I was told to get in touch with someone here — I was told he would be able to — '

I stopped. There was something about the woman's expression that made me feel cruelly embarrassed, as if I had asked why a cripple limped or a blind man stumbled.

'This is a home for down-and-outers, I suppose. They hear about us, or someone delivers them and leaves them on the doorstep. We're a private foundation. Very poor. We help people who can't help themselves any more. Worthwhile people, all of them.' She smiled a little in the gloom; I felt an onrush of sheer misery. 'There are some men — and a few women too — for whom the Welfare State can't find an answer. All with problems that can't always be defined. Drink, drugs, they're common, but we have worse to cope with. Why not come inside and then perhaps we can talk more? You did want to see somebody here?'

'He's Ruane,' I said. 'Is he one of those here for help?'

'Yes.'

'But I was told to come to him for help!'

'All the more reason for you to come

inside,' she said. 'Out of the chill.'

I thought: you phoney, Schofield. You bastard! He had sent me halfway across the country to see a drunk or a drug-addict at a decrepit house in the middle of nowhere. Bitter anger gave me back my self-control.

The woman said. 'I'll tell Mr. Ruane he has a visitor. He'll be pleased.'

'Why is he here?' I asked.

'Why don't you ask him? He is a good and kind man,' she said. 'I'm told that he went through a terrible experience and that it left him with spiritual and psychological handicaps almost too great to be borne. But he lived with them and he has used his gifts to aid those in even worse trouble than himself. If he reverts to the anodyne that helps him cope with his damaged mind, who can blame him?'

'I've never met him, I don't know anything about him!'

I could hardly see her face, but I sensed amusement was there. 'Come in,' she said.

I followed her.

The rooms were clean, but the

furniture was shabby; I had seen places like this around the centre of London. I could smell poverty, old age, stale cooking smells, suffering and the fear of loneliness; that, and the body-smells of people who wore cast-offs. The corridors were carpeted in a threadbare Axminster; the damp patches on the walls showed through the bright new paint.

We stopped at a door on the east wing of the house.

'We're two or even three to a room, but Mr. Ruane's lucky. He's not had to share at the moment.' She knocked at the door. 'I'm a sort of warden. Jacqueline Page.'

'Anne Blackwell,' I said. What was this Ruane?

There was no answer. 'He may be asleep,' said the woman. She knocked again. 'Mr. Ruane?'

A man's voice answered. 'Coming.' It was a deep voice, and though muffled by the intervening door, it was obviously that of an educated man.

The door opened a few inches, and I saw the man called Ruane. I saw the heavy drinker's features and the jowls and

I caught the stench of alcohol fumes as soon as the doors opened. I felt sick with shame for him and for myself, this latter because I had been naive enough to listen to Schofield.

Ruane had been a heavily built man: now he was gross, He had the small forehead, the grizzled curly hair, the porcine nose and watery blue eyes in a great red face, and the bull neck and heavy sloping shoulders of the Irish peasant. He looked at me and turned away.

'Miss Blackwell has driven from London to see you,' said the Page woman.

'She can come in if she wishes,' he said, but he would not look at me,

'Talk to him,' said the woman very quietly. I wondered at the insistence. 'He knew you were coming,' she added.

I was startled into silence. I had my excuses for retreating ready prepared. I left them unspoken. Ruane knew Charles Schofield: or, rather, Charles Schofield had recommended that I talk to Ruane. And the Page woman was aware of the connection.

I took fresh stock of her. Maybe she was more than she seemed. There are still many upper-middle-class women who engage in public service, sacrificing themselves and their fortunes if the cause seems to warrant it.

She could know Schofield.

Where did Ruane fit in?

I had nothing to lose by talking to him, I decided.

I entered the room and was repulsed by the stench. It was some kind of grape product.

'I'll leave you for a while,' said Jacqueline Page. Ruane didn't acknowledge her.

I looked about me, without hiding my feelings. Apart from the body stench of the man, who was wearing what looked like someone's cast-off suit and a greasy cardigan, there was the odour of neglect about the room. The bed was unmade and the sheets unclean.

Ruane saw my disgust.

'It's filthy,' he said quietly, swaying slightly.

Then I saw the one ornament.

It was a crucifix maybe two foot in height, hung on the wall beside the unmade bed. It was rough-cut from beech, a fine piece of work, but the face and torso were unusual, for Christ was not the elegant muscled athlete of the typical agony: he was a broad and bowed and contorted figure, built like a wrestler; the face was heavy, not fine-boned and Semitic. The pain was fearful in that brutal face.

Ruane watched me. He slurred his words, but I heard them plainly. 'Don't make assumptions,' he said. 'A friend who is now dead carved it for me. He was blind from birth. But what sort of Christ could a blind man see?'

There was something about Ruane's swaying figure, about the seedy room, and about the crucifix that unbalanced me.

'What use is someone like you!' I yelled. 'For God's sake, I've driven from London to see you!'

Ruane looked away. He was only holding himself up with difficulty.

'Tell me what use it was!' I screamed.

'None,' he mumbled. 'None for any of

us. Not for the living, and not for the one I couldn't help before, God rest his soul.' He crossed himself, and I heard a few words from a prayer.

Tears splashed down my face. Ruane's great red face turned slowly in my direction. Then he looked at his right hand, which was raised in benediction. There was a bottle of cheap brandy in it.

When he saw the bottle, his expression changed. First he clenched his teeth and growled in a deep rasping voice, words that were incomprehensible. Then his arm went back.

For a moment I thought he intended to hurl it at me. His expression changed again when he saw me cowering away from him.

Quite clearly, and in an educated voice, he said:

'Why did you come to me?'

'Someone has to help me!' I said hopelessly.

'Help?' He looked at the bottle and gulped a mouthful of brandy. He gagged on it. but kept it down. 'I helped someone before. I faced the Devil — and there is a

Devil! And a Hell! And there are those who serve the Evil One, believe me!'

He began moaning quietly, but I couldn't hear the words. When he stopped I said loudly:

'I'm talking about Monteine Castle!' I was too tired now to change my mind about telling him the story. I had maybe three or four minutes to get something across to him, then he'd be unconscious for as many hours.

'I'm talking about evil,' he said, blinking back into coherency only with an effort.

'I am too!'

We faced one another like antagonists.

He peered blearily at me. 'Go back to where you came from!' he said.

'You know about evil, Ruane!' I yelled.

'Evil?' he said, his watery eyes focusing at last. 'Evil. It grows, and then there is the death of the soul.'

I started again. Very directly, I said:

'An evil man called Simon Miaolo has some kind of hold over my fiancé. He is Richard Ulrome, There's a connection between him and Monteine Castle. His ancestors are buried there. He doesn't seem to be aware that he goes down to the family crypt most nights. I think he's drugged. They're setting him up for some diabolical happening — I know! I can sense it.'

Ruane closed his eyes and lurched back as if I had hit him.

He recovered, and I yelled at him:

'It's to happen on Lammas Eve! On Saturday!'

Ruane blinked and looked at me.

There was a flicker of intelligence now in the strange deep eyes. He dropped the bottle. It fell with a dull thud, and the stench of the cheap brandy filled the room. A thin coil of the liquid reached out towards me. Ruane pointed with the hand now free.

He mumbled something, words I couldn't catch.

I leaned forward, sure that at last he was to tell me something: such is hope. I had never lost my belief in Charles Schofield, not really; Freda had never been wrong about men. Surely?

'How can I get Richard away?' I whispered.

The words came out thick and harsh:

'At Lammas — tide — the evil thing — '

'Yes? What!' I knew he was near telling me something of great importance. I willed him to speak.

' — the ancient evil — ' he grated, and then he steadied himself against the wall. 'Keep away! Keep away!'

'Keep away from what? Here? Monteine? I don't understand!'

The eyes emptied of expression, Ruane's heavy torso buckled and slowly he subsided to the floor. He didn't harm himself. It was as natural and easy a fall as a dog lying down.

And this wreck, I asked myself, my thoughts swinging violently from pity to fury, from trust to a total and disbelieving detestation of the man, this hulk could envisage engaging in *God's work*?

I felt like kicking him.

13

I couldn't have driven back to London, but the night in a Norwich hotel didn't bring me much rest. I wished at about half-past four in the morning that I had never met Richard. Love can be a colossal burden.

He had allowed me to become entangled in his life; he had reached out and made me a part of him. And, just when I was sure of myself, after so many years of self-deception and self-mistrust, he had taken it all away. I fell asleep for a couple of hours at that point, and when I awoke I remembered all my anguished thoughts.

I ran a cold shower and kept myself under it for a minute. I felt better. After dressing, I had time for a quick breakfast before checking out of the hotel, and driving back to London.

Ruane had turned out to be useless. I didn't blame Charles Schofield; he couldn't have known that the man he had sent me to was now a drink-sodden wreck.

So what could I do?

Go to New York, I told myself. And, once there, enquire into the circumstances of the death of Richard's relative, the Ulrome who had been the fifteenth Earl of Monteine

And after that?

God knew, but I might have some information with which to convince Richard that he was being manipulated by Miaolo's gang. It was Wednesday; I had until Saturday to work things out. Then, if all else failed, only direct confrontation was left, whatever the consequences.

As I continued the drive to London, I found myself able to shut a door in my mind on the eerie events at Monteine Castle, and concentrate on the things I had to do. Saturday was a long time away.

I had a busy schedule. First I called at the American Embassy. They had my visa ready; a charming young woman said I'd be very welcome in her country. I hoped so. Then I thought: Who is De Vito? Firmly I told myself not to speculate.

I remembered other things I had to do when I got back to my flat, and I did them with efficiency. I put off a couple of artists. I made sure that a small publishing house I'd sold work to knew they were two months late with their cheque; I'd need money soon, for the air-ticket wiped out most of my current bank balance. I rang Gloria. Tony was in excellent health, she said. He was out with the family across the way. They were all going to the seaside for the day; Gloria began to ask about Richard, but I switched the subject to her loft conversion. I listened to her enthusiasm, checking my reservation for the Kennedy flight and rang Bill Marr.

'I tried a dozen times to get you, darling!' he said.

'I had some out-of-town appointments. Did you get anything for me, Bill?'

'Jackpot!' he said. 'You've no idea what a fascinating family the Ulromes are. I make it one beheading for treason, a touch of religious mania in the early eighteenth century, leading to suicide; and two glorious deaths in battle on the losing side. They were an impulsive lot, the Ulromes. Of course, I've left the titillating bit till last, and this one's not well documented at all — it looks as though the family's done almost a totally effective job of destroying contemporary documents so far as the sixth Earl is concerned. Lots of nasty suspicions and a gory little legend. How does that grab you, darling?'

'Badly, Bill. Give me a moment.'

'There's more, but this is geographical detail. You know there's a tectonic fault line running through that part of the wilds?'

'What!'

'I forget. You never were into the environment. All right, I'll make it simple. Anne, that part of North Yorkshire's coast is subject to minor tremors from deep displacements maybe twenty miles down. You don't get cities falling apart, but earthquake tremors have been recorded up to 5.7 on the Richter scale. That means buildings can be damaged, and that's what happened in part to the Monteine estate.'

What to say, what to make of it, and did it matter, I found myself asking. Maybe. This was just a natural phenomenon, though. So, they caught a bit of discomfort and maybe the pots fell off the mantelpiece and a few stones got knocked about. So?

'Bill. Yes? And?'

'There was a biggish shaker about two hundred years ago. The main buildings survived intact, but some of the outlying properties were damaged. The chapel caught it, mainly, so the records state. The incumbent of the local church set it out precisely. One Nicodemus Platt, the rev. You there still, Anne?'

I didn't wish to know any more about minor disasters. My concern was with more unnatural griefs. Richard, in deadly peril. Stones falling, the earth shaking, what was that?

'Tell me about the sixth Earl, Bill.'

'Too long a story — hints here and there, a bit of a cross-reference in the standard guides to folklore for the area. I put photocopies of all relevant extracts in the post. Haven't you got them yet?'

My letterbox was in the hall; the postman wouldn't deliver to individual flats.

'I haven't looked, Bill.'

'Have dinner with me tonight?'

'I wish I could,' I said honestly. 'But I'm going to New York this afternoon.'

'Is Ulrome there?'

'No! He's at — He's looking at a boat in Yorkshire.'

As Bill gave me a brief outline of the evidence he had uncovered, I felt a deep, cold certainty about the evil that was being planned. Things were fitting together, the ancient legend and the events I had witnessed at Monteine Castle.

'I've got it right, have I?' I asked, 'Was the sixth Earl a Satanist?'

'You'll have to judge for yourself from the evidence, darling. I can't put my hand on my heart and say that the sixteenth-century sixth Earl of Monteine was in league with the Devil, which, as all nice girls should know, is the classical definition of a Satanist. No! That he dabbled in the occult — yes. That the local legends credit him with diabolical powers — yes. That somewhere he fits into the folklore of the region as some kind of monster — again yes. Very much yes on all three counts, darling. But there's so little evidence that one can't swear anything but that the Earl lived, that he died, and that he's buried at Monteine Castle in the family vault. Now, if I find anything else, I'll tell you. But just answer one question, will you, Anne? I'd have thought this kind of nastiness was best left to historians. So why the interest in this family? It just isn't your style. Why dig it up?'

'Why? A girl wants to know what she's getting into, doesn't she?'

He agreed, but he was still curious about me when at last he rang off. I went to collect the packet he had sent; it was there, a thick sheaf of stiff papers. I flicked through them, but I couldn't concentrate; there was time enough on the flight to read in detail what Bill Marr had outlined.

I still had a little time in hand so I rang

Freda, but she was out. I wanted to talk to someone who knew me well and again hear that Charles Schofield was a man whose judgments could be relied on; after that I did what I had wanted to do for hours. I rang through to Monteine Castle. I got through to a secretary, a very brisk woman, who passed me on to Monica Sievel. She said she thought Richard had gone for a walk, or maybe he was in the village pub. She wanted to know about London — what was the weather like, were the sales worth visiting, what shows had I seen, all in her kindly sly manner. They weren't going to put me through to Richard, but I persisted until my patience ran out.

'As a matter of fact, I'll be out of London for a day or two,' I said. 'Yes, I'm flying to New York this afternoon.'

A small pause, then she said:

'Why, that's marvellous, dear! I suppose it's some artistic commission?'

'It is business,' I said, and I was angry and afraid. 'For Richard.'

'He's lucky to have a capable girl like you!'

She was ready now with her clever question, but I knew how to cut off a conversation. I said she should tell Richard I'd called and put the phone down. I half-hoped I detected a note of alarm in her voice, and then I felt scared again. I was going to New York to find out if they had killed an old man. I couldn't lock the doors of my mind however much I tried, and I put off reading the Ulrome papers until I was on the Kennedy jet.

14

The long flight to New York gave me plenty of time to study the contents of the report Bill Marr had sent me.

I had waited until the American next to me had gone to sleep before I opened the packet. I couldn't have concentrated on the weird, macabre and frightening accounts with someone watching my every move. He snored but at least he wouldn't interrupt me.

I skimmed Bill Marr's note: it was polite and academic and clever. I pursed my lips, then reminded myself that Bill had put time and effort into helping, and that I was an ungrateful bitch, the more so since he had typed an index to the extracts. Those concerned with the sixth Earl were clipped together. I had no interest in the rest of the material; I think Bill had guessed that. The small archaic print of the first extract swam before my eyes. I picked out phrases here and there:

'a horrible-shaped thing', and 'as it were of his clawes or talans'.

It was here before me, the mystery I had to resolve. Impatiently I flicked the pages over, then I came to one that glared at me. The last sheet was a copy of a very old engraving, not well executed, but plain enough: it was a massive stone tomb. I had last seen it only two days before in the burial-chamber of the Earls of Monteine. There could be no mistaking that grim carven tomb, for the light in the crypt had been quite strong enough for me to have fixed its shape and proportions on my memory, just as I could recall the frozen, cruel expression on Richard's face.

I read Bill Marr's typed note with a growing sense of horror:

'I couldn't make out the inscription on the tomb, but it seems to tie in with the MacIver note. What a nasty man our Neville de Burgh Ulrome was!'

MacIver?

There were only four lines. A curiosity seeker called Alexander MacIver had compiled a book of sayings, inscriptions and epitaphs, which he found in Northumberland and Yorkshire. All that he had written about the Ulromes was that one Neville de Burgh Ulrome, who had died in 1585, had left a warning to those who disturbed his rest.

'Not unusual,' Bill Marr had written, 'but this is unpleasantly explicit. I've translated it for you because of the Latin's bad medieval grammar.'

Bill Marr's translation made me shudder. The long dead Earl had warned: 'Disturb me at your peril when you call the power from the sea'.

Bill had added another note. ' 'Power' isn't right in this context. It's more like 'malignancy' or 'evil', but there's no direct equivalent for the local term. If anything, it's more like the parish priest's wording in the older extract. Interesting stuff,' he ended.

I knew it was evil, malignant and that it had power, for I had seen the rearing horrible shape at Monteine Castle. But what was all this to Richard?

Feverishly I read on. The longest account was that of an unnamed priest of the church of St. Michael in the parish of Monteine. It was dated 1586. The start was riveting:

'A straunge and terrible Wunder wrought very late in the parish of Monteine, in ye yeere of our Lord 1586, in a great tempest of violent raine, lightning and thunder, the like whereof hath been seldome seene. With the appearance of a horrible shaped thing, running from the sea on to the cliffes with great swiftness, and incredible haste in a visible fourm and shape, in the dayes of August at the time of Lammas-fest.'

'Now for the verifying of this report (which to some will seem absurd, although the sensiblenesse of the thing it self confirmeth it to be a trueth) as testimonies and witnesses of the force which rested in this straunge shaped thing, there are remaining in the stones of the cliff, and likewise in the chapel dore which are mervelously renten and torne, ye marks as it were of his clawes or talans.'

There was more, but it was religious speculation on the reasons for this visitation. Bill Marr again had added a note: 'The Ulromes probably had most contemporary accounts suppressed. This story survived in the personal papers of the priest'.

Later Ulromes, more respectable Earls of Monteine, would not wish such macabre legends in their history. I wondered when they had walled up the ancient crypt, then the big aircraft shook slightly, bringing a welcome distraction. 'Nothing to be concerned about,' our pilot assured us. 'A slight change of engine pitch, ladies and gentlemen.' I read on. There was one frightful little extract left.

Half a century after the death of the sixth Earl, someone had been on the cliffs late at night, again at the beginning of August. Two torn bodies lay in white moonlight, both strangers. A black, evil shape had been seen by an anonymous informant; the description was shockingly effective. I couldn't bring myself to reread it, but one phrase kept clanging around my mind with an iron force: 'no shape of living creature, a deadlie thing . . . '

I got a couple of hours' sleep and woke

up utterly dejected when the plane landed at Kennedy Airport.

We'd gained time on the crossing. It wasn't mid-evening, as it should have been by the clock in my brain; in New York, they were just finishing work for the day.

There was tremendous bustle at the airport: it was holiday time. I'd already thought out what I'd say to the immigration officials when they asked the purpose of my visit. I told the pleasantly spoken youngish man that I was looking up some business contacts. He looked concerned about me. I was getting used to that rather odd look people were giving me: as if they thought I wasn't quite right in the head.

The terminal buildings were packed with noisy family groups. I pushed through to a payphone. John de Vito's number unsurprisingly turned out to be that of a precinct-station in a busy downtown commercial sector. I asked for him. The female operator asked me to hold, then passed me on to the Duty Sergeant.

'Who's calling, please?' I was asked. I

said I was from England and gave my name. Where was I? At Kennedy. Before I got another question out I was invited to go over right away: firmly but pleasantly. I was to be sure to ask for the right address. He got me to repeat it, said I was doing fine, then the line went dead.

I assumed that Charles Schofield's contact had been expecting me, and that he'd left a message with the Duty Sergeant. Lieutenant John de Vito would perhaps be on call somewhere. I should have known enough by then to assume nothing. I still had hope.

I looked at the thick neck of the coloured driver and dropped into a near sleep which was dominated by another phrase from the ancient account: 'for that they were direly torn', I shuddered awake as I watched the chaos of the huge city slide by my dark glass windows. It had the appearance of a dream; the reality was the insubstantial malignancy at Monteine. I forced myself to be alert as the cab stopped.

The place looked like a police station — eight storeys of it, greyish concrete and as functional as a gas stove. Two elderly, complaining women pushed through the glass doors as I entered.

A policeman in shirtsleeves came to the desk when I had waited a few minutes. Behind him, a big blond-haired man also in shirtsleeves but not in police uniform, was munching sandwiches. I realized that I was hungry myself. The desk officer pointed at the airline bag I'd brought my overnight things in.

'Lady, would you mind placing that grip on the desk?'

'I've come to see Lieutenant de Vito,' I said. 'My name is Anne Blackwell. If you'll tell Lieutenant de Vito that I'm here, you can make a detailed inventory.' I was too tired to argue, to work out why the wretched bag had offended him.

I caught an interested look from the man with the sandwich. He got to his feet. He was bigger than I had imagined, blond-haired, hard, about forty. 'I don't mind at all if you look in the grip,' I said to the desk man.

He was a youngish sergeant, very sure of himself. 'It's regulations, lady,' he said, as he unzipped the bag. 'You wouldn't believe how many nuts we get in here with an arsenal in their luggage.'

'Excuse me, you're Miss Blackwell?' asked the big man.

'Yes.'

'I've been waiting to meet you.' He grinned at the desk sergeant. 'No hardware?'

'Nothing that shouldn't be there, Lieutenant,' the sergeant said, 'I'll leave you to the Lieutenant, Miss.'

I smiled at the sergeant. I didn't like having my things looked over, but he had been discreet. I said something about Englishwomen being notorious gun molls, and John de Vito smiled approval.

He slipped his jacket on, a light tweed in a Hebridean weave and design I admired. He was aware of my gaze, I saw, for he looked at the lapel of his jacket; and then I saw the pin in the buttonhole. It had a bright enamel icon, an xyz . . . (Knights of St. Columbia) . . .

I had the strongest sensation of intrusion just then. So I did not make any comment, either about the jacket, and certainly not about the pin. But I was aware of its significance.

'Good trip?' he asked.

'Good enough, Lieutenant,' I said. 'It's good of you to be here to meet me.'

De Vito nodded. 'You're tired, you're hungry, and you need a drink. Bill,' he called to the sergeant at the desk, 'if I'm needed, call Rugantmo's. I guess you passed up the airline food?' he asked me as he led me through the lobby, 'I don't blame you. Can you eat pasta?'

The place he took me to was part-bar, part-restaurant. We ate informally in a small booth; I had the house lasagna, and accepted a drink.

'Feel like talking now?' de Vito said, as I mopped up the sauce with some bread.

'I expect Charles Schofield explained the hurry, Lieutenant. How much did he tell you?'

'Not much.'

'No, I suppose he wouldn't, not over the phone.'

'So tell it,' he said.

'It's about a man called Miaolo. Simon Miaolo. He's mixed up in some sort of devilry.'

'Where?'

'In England. On the North Yorkshire coast. There's a small fishing town called Monteine Landing. Miaolo's oil company has a U.K. promotions and research centre at Monteine Castle. That's where Miaolo's going.'

'And where do you come into this?'

'I don't. My fiancé does. Didn't Charles Schofield tell you about him?'

'I want to hear it from you.'

'My fiancé is Richard Ulrome. I heard Kresak talking about him.'

De Vito's expression showed a sudden interest, 'So it's Kresak and Miaolo?'

'And the man who died here two weeks ago. He was an Ulrome too. By his death Richard became the sixteenth Earl of Monteine. Miaolo is preparing some kind of occult experiment involving Richard. And the death of the old Earl. Don't you see, it has to be connected!'

'How do you know?' He was clearly interested now.

'I heard them!' Encouraged by his interest, I said: 'I know you wouldn't talk to me under normal circumstances, but I have to know about the old Earl. What did happen?'

De Vito frowned. He looked down at his big hands. 'Kresak. No question about it. But a very careful and clever piece of butchery, no clues, not a sign of a killing. But it was done. You want to know how?'

'No!'

I had enough on my mind without the thought of the gruesome incidental details.

'Just tell me why you believe Miaolo was concerned — please,' I said. 'I have to be sure in my own mind that you're right before I can persuade Richard that it was a killing.'

De Vito poured coffee for us.

'All right, Anne. I've seen the results of Miaolo's work before. Kresak was always involved.'

'He frightens me, this Kresak. What is he?'

'A killer. Professional. Latvian, so our files say. Multi-lingual, worked for one of the Communist intelligence agencies. Big, dark, very smooth. Eyes like a shark's. Miaolo bought him out of the business, made sure he was safe, keeps him loyal with the prospect of inheriting a chunk of the International empire. Anyway he likes the work.'

'Is he over here now?' I asked.

'Leave Kresak out of this,' he said, with an air of finality. His face had taken on a hard look. 'Tell me the rest of your story.'

So I told him. All of it. My first visit to the Castle. The dinner party. My drinking, and the details of the stories. And then, with a desperation that came through to de Vito, for he ordered brandy at that point, I began to tell him about the cliff walk to the chapel. Again I relived the horrific moments in the tower room; and the awful moments in the chapel. I felt my skin crawling, even with the warmth of the brandy spreading its glow through my body.

I came to the morning awakening, and I felt afraid once more. I could see the hair on the back of John de Vito's big hands — despite his name, he was light-haired, not a Latin at all — and the sight of the light dusting of hair brought me to a point near terror.

'I told myself I'd imagined it,' I said. 'But it was there. I felt a line of bristly fur. Harsh black fur on his back. And when I looked in the mirror the second time at Monteine he wasn't there! He wasn't! There was something else hovering behind him! There was! God help me, there was!'

I began to sob until I caught a glance from John de Vito.

'Keep talking.' His solid, calm acceptance held me together.

So I told him about the three psychologists or whatever they were, and about Kresak's instructions. I described the silent progress along the cliffs, and as I told him, I could see him picturing the black sea and the sheen of the stars, and the moonlight making a wide silver track over the heaving waves. I was completely in control of myself by the time I had finished.

He nodded. 'You said you saw a television broadcast. Let me ask one thing now, and consider it carefully. First, a man called Kresak said that in that particular situation you could be a catalyst. We both know what they meant. They believed you would soften Richard up, affect him in some way, so that they could more easily and more effectively gain control of him? Right?' He didn't wait for an answer.

'Now, consider the question of the television broadcast and think carefully. Were you meant to overhear it?'

It hadn't occurred to me that they could be so devious. I was appalled.

'No. They couldn't have known I'd switch the television set on. It was accidental.'

I didn't know what to think by now, but I'd decided to believe that it was an accident. And the eavesdropping too: they didn't know about either occurrence.

How could they?

'I think you're right,' said de Vito. Before I could ask why, he went on: 'You're here, aren't you?'

And, when he waited for a moment, I understood. I could be on the black rocks now. If they had any reason to suspect that I was seeking help, they would have killed me by now.

'Oh no,' I said.

A waiter beckoned de Vito.

'Pardon me,' he said. 'I guess it's the station-house.'

He'd told the desk sergeant where to contact him. I needed a few moments to myself anyway. The dark-haired waiter came over.

'You like the pasta?'

'Wonderful. Could you get me another brandy, please. And one for Lieutenant de Vito.'

The grin vanished.

'Say who, lady?'

I was watching John de Vito at the phone. His face was serious,

'The Lieutenant.' I pointed. 'Lieutenant de Vito.'

The waiter had that pitying, slightly awed look I had learned to hate.

'You got it wrong, lady. That's the guy's buddy, I mean, you know about de Vito, sure you know, lady!'

'I do? What about him?'

'So he got unlucky.'

I knew then de Vito was dead. The cold evil had lapped over me again. It had claimed a good man.

'Hit and run lady — some old motor, a Caddy, they say hell, no one really saw — '

'When?'

'Last night. Mass at St. Peter's just along 11th at eight this morning. Big turn out. All the Knights at the precinct house for sure.'

Of course.

Another Roman Catholic connection. The waiter saw the intensity of my gaze and took heed of my fright. I began to panic.

'I've got to go,' I heard myself saying.

'Now look, lady, Joe Leckov won't like this at all, sure he won't.' He was looking at the blond-haired Lieutenant who had lied to me — but had he? Had he claimed to be de Vito? 'I get the brandies, uh?'

'Do that.'

He was still talking into the phone. I didn't need to work it out rationally. Another death, one more accident. He hadn't claimed to be de Vito, he'd just gone along with my ready acceptance of him as the man I expected to be waiting for me. I'd said he was John de Vito, he'd taken it from there, He was entitled to carry out his investigation into his friend's killing in any way that happened along. His was a grudge-fight, against Kresak and Miaolo. But it wasn't my fight.

This big man wouldn't help me save Richard, his interest was with the death of his friend de Vito. They wanted Miaolo's hatchet man, Kresak, and I was the only lead they had. Kresak had been in New York, I was sure of it. I couldn't hate Joe Leckov, not at all. I knew, though, that he'd try to keep me in New York. There was a category of persons called 'material witnesses', hadn't we all watched American movies? Joe Leckov's next step would have been to persuade me to stay over. If persuasion didn't work I'd be held in custody, very politely, but still with a locked door.

I waved to him until I caught his attention. I smiled a false smile and pointed to what was labelled as a Comfort Room; I had the wit to leave my overnight case, to confuse and delay him. My passport and visa, my tickets and money were in my handbag. I waved cheerfully and sidled out of his range of vision. I had an hour's start. I didn't think it would take me long to get out of Kennedy — for all their boasted efficiency, their police forces aren't supermen.

I was going back to England.

There was nothing for me in the United States. I tried not to curse Charles Schofield, but it was hard going. I felt so alone that I looked at other people as if they were all dead and myself the last person alive in the entire world.

So I made the wrong choice, and it wasn't until it was all over that I learned that this big, solid, grieving officer of the law had done all the right things, despite my half-crazed decision to abandon him. He was not alone in this.

15

Nothing went wrong. I transferred to a British Airways flight with no trouble at all. It left at midnight local time and when I arrived at Heathrow I knew what I had to do. There was enough time. Tomorrow night was Lammas Eve, and I had a whole day in which to arrange matters. I had managed to sleep on the return flight. It was under-booked, so I had four adjacent seats to myself; a stewardess suggested I stretch out. When we landed I was still tired and shivery, though I wasn't at all weak; I was fairly sure that desperation would see me through; I had nothing else. I'd been away for not much more than twenty-four hours. It seemed almost incredible that I had crossed the Atlantic twice in that time.

It was raining heavily, the wind pounding the glass and concrete. I took a taxi from the airport, not something I would have done normally; but I felt that

I had something to gain by hurrying.

By the time I got back to the flat, I was less tense. I flipped through the mail, wondering if Richard had written. He hadn't but then he hated writing anyway.

'It's tomorrow night,' I heard myself saying. I saw myself in the small mirror in the hall. I looked ghastly.

I went into the lounge and stared out at the park where a small boy was playing by himself. I wanted to see my son, then, right away. I had to be sure of something, so I went to the phone and picked up the receiver.

I was about to ring Gloria's number when the door-chimes jangled. Richard? That was my first thought. Gloria? Then, chillingly, Kresak?

Whoever it was knocked at the door. Nervously, I put the receiver down and went to open it.

I saw the big red face and smelt the alcohol. I started to slam the door, but Ruane's big arm held it firmly open.

'Get away!' I hissed, glad to have a focus for my anger. 'You — '

'I'm cold,' he said, in that soft,

drinker's voice with a hint of brogue in it, for I knew the accent now. 'It was cold waiting.'

He had the same ill-fitting suit on, but no overcoat. His clothes were soaked. His grizzled hair was plastered to his large skull. He was shivering.

I felt ashamed of my anger, then the desperation flooded through me and I was furious, just as I had been at the home for derelicts, but curiously I could pity him too. I wanted him to go away, but I couldn't turn him out into the rain. It took me a minute or two to work out that he had left the miserable Fenland house when he had slept off the brandy.

He waited until I summed up the situation. He looked utterly fatigued, yet he stood straight enough. Though he was shivering with alcoholic withdrawal, there was a steady intelligence about him that altogether confused me.

'How long have you been waiting?'

He shrugged. 'It doesn't matter.'

'Did Charles Schofield give you my address? And how did you get here — by train? Bus?'

'Something like that.'

He was still waiting patiently for me to make up my mind to ask him in.

'So you walked?'

'Not all the way. People are kind on the road.'

'Did Miss Page send you?'

'No.'

I believed him.

'You've come to help me?'

'If I can.'

'You'd better come in.' I couldn't turn him out into the rain, not right away, but I couldn't allow myself to hope for help from anyone.

I pointed to a chair. 'Please sit down. I'll turn the electric fire on. Have a brandy, that'll warm you.'

I said it without thought.

Ruane smiled bleakly. 'Maybe not.'

He sat down and huddled forward to take the heat of the three electric bars.

'I'm sorry,' I said. 'At your house you couldn't face me, that's right, isn't it?'

Ruane rubbed his hands together slowly. There were mud streaks on his clothes where he had slept in ditches.

He saw my unease.

'Would you make a tired old man a cup of coffee?' he asked quietly.

He wasn't really old, but he was making it easy for me.

'I will,' I said. 'I could find you a blanket whilst your clothes dried.'

'I'll be fine in a few minutes.' He looked better already. 'But thank you.'

I had bacon and eggs and coffee ready in a few minutes. He didn't object when I brought the tray in. He had stopped shivering by that time, and the flat was full of the stench of his clothes. He took the tray from me and ate steadily, but fast. Probably he hadn't any money to buy food.

I noticed the parcel he had been carrying. It was something wrapped in newspaper, about two feet long, not wide. He saw the direction of my gaze as he finished eating.

He was ready to talk. With a quick and deft movement of his big hands, he pulled the wet newspaper away. I had half-guessed what it would be.

It was the blind man's rough-made crucifix.

Ruane passed it to me, and, without pausing to consider what I was doing or why, I ran my palm over the squat, pain-twisted wooden torso. I hadn't felt a moment of religious belief since my early teens, but I experienced something in that moment that at once made me wince with hope, I said:

'You've been a priest?'

Ruane met my gaze. 'I once had that privilege. Now I serve where I can. Badly, and with great fear, and always against my better judgment, but I try to serve.'

'So you were Father Ruane?'

'Ruane is just a name I use,' he said quietly. 'I don't pretend it's my own. God forgive me. I rejected my calling and I'll have no questioning about it. It's finished, and there's no looking back, not in this life.'

Against my will, he was affecting me, this man who came out of the rain. Even with that calm, almost graceful manner, he was still a man rejected by his church, and apparently for good cause.

Undoubtedly, Ruane had come to offer help. Otherwise, why carry a crucifix

200

across half of England and wait for hours in the streaming rain for a woman he had met only once, and that when he was only semi-conscious.

'Do you know why I came to Norfolk?'

'Because of Simon Miaolo.'

Despite my compassion, I was still adversely affected by the stench and the sight of him, 'I don't need *you*!' I blurted.

He grabbed my arm.

'Sit down! Here, beside me, and listen for a few minutes. No, listen!' he said harshly as I struggled. 'Woman, you're as arrogant as you're helpless! I'm useless in all things but the one that crazes you, so you'll sit and listen if I have to hold you down!'

I told him I'd listen if he'd release me.

He didn't make apologies for his show of force. He told me, very simply, about an Irish peasant boy who had known he was destined for the priesthood from his earliest years; about the years of toil, the effort to apply a hitherto untutored mind to the sternest of all disciplines; and the years of pastoral care.

He was talking about himself, I

realized. He left a gap in the story and pointed to another figure. Middle-aged, derelict, bitterly aggrieved at himself and all he had once been.

There were years of desperate solitude, and degradation, yet somehow he had kept himself and a remnant of faith alive.

He came to his senses one night in a Midlands town. 'I heard the voice of evil,' he said simply. 'At night, it was. Clear and loud and gloating, and I knew there was a dried husk of a soulless devil loose in the town. Something so evil, so terrible, that it would rip and rage until it had eaten its way into any number of souls, and become a great and monstrous force in the land. I heard it, and I knew enough to act.'

'You?' I said disbelievingly.

'Before God, I acted in the way I knew best! I ripped the evil from the women's bodies, but though the devil went back to the Hell it came from, a good man died that night!'[1]

I felt cold. There was so much of agony

---

[1] *Mark of the Beast*.

in Ruane that it chilled me to the bone. But I couldn't turn him away. Disbelieving, desperate, almost without the will to hope, nevertheless I began to trust him.

After a long silence, he said:

'I went for advice and comfort to the holiest man I have ever known. He was a saintly man who had seen the worst of humankind, and he was not without experience of the things that we call satanic powers.'

I felt the man's powerful aura. He radiated power now. The gross figure was only the outer shell of the man's spiritual force. Ruane, whatever he might have done, had power. Far more than any other man I had seen, except, I thought with a shudder, the terrible Simon Miaolo.

'He told me how I should spend my life,' Ruane went on. 'He said I was one of the few to whom it was given to be able to detect evil, the true evil that is unknown to the most part of humanity. Deathless, cold, angry evil, without home or hope, mankind's endless enemy, which seeks to devour the souls of men.'

He looked at me with a terrible compassion.

'When you came, I knew,' he said.

'About Simon Miaolo? And the legends of Monteine? Yes, that's it, you've heard of the Ulromes and the chapel! See, it's all down here!'

I passed him Bill Marr's file.

'Oh, yes, Charles Schofield was right! You know about Miaolo — that's why you came, to me!'

He shook his head.

'My gift is to detect evil.' He didn't take the papers from me. 'You didn't need these. You could sense the evil, couldn't you?'

I was trembling with horror.

'Yes!'

'You have the gift too.'

'I don't know anything!'

'You were there. You saw, smelt, sought out the evil. They knew it. I've no doubt that they used you.'

A catalyst. They knew it. Jensen, Fitch, Sievel. And the smiling killer Kresak. Somehow, they had known that I would sense what they were about, and they had used me. Against Richard.

Whatever power Ruane had possessed, belonged to me in some small way. And I had been used to affect Richard.

How?

'Some people, not many, have a perception of things that seem to most beyond reality. But they are real,' said Ruane.

'And you knew when you saw me that they were dabbling in — in — '

'In the worst thing of all,' finished Ruane. 'I sensed it when you were coming. And, to my shame, I denied you. Forgive me?'

'Yes!'

Ruane got to his feet,

'Then it's time I learned all there is to know about this business.'

We talked at length, questions and answers, conjecture and summary, until Ruane knew all that I had so far learned about the Ulromes and their mysterious association with the evil at Monteine; and about the man who had killed and killed again to ensure that no one interfered with his equally mysterious designs, and my own only half-understood place in those designs.

I understood so much more when I was through.

16

'So I'm psychic?' I asked, when I had finished.

'Call it what you like,' Ruane said, 'you have what the educated refer to as extrasensory perception; where I came from it is called the evil eye. It's something of a shock, isn't it?'

'They sent me with Richard to the chapel because of it.' I wasn't asking a question. I knew. 'And my influence made him see the fallen stone as a carven head.'

'It was convenient for them that you turned up. They're resourceful. You have a strong psychic aura, and Richard was closer to you than anyone else,' Ruane agreed 'You yourself were the medium. They knew it at once, of course. I've no doubt that all the principals at the Castle were selected for their skill in the occult, and particularly for their sensitivity to supernatural presences. The one you call Jensen, now. I have a feeling I have heard of him before. I travelled a good deal as a young man,' Ruane explained. 'There isn't a club to equal the priesthood for the exchange of information. We know most of the trade in evil. Devilry and all its manifestations are a part of our trade.'

'What shall I do?'

'First we must ascertain exactly how the misguided creatures at Monteine are planning to use Richard Ulrome.'

'You mean you don't know? But I thought now that you had all the information about the — the beast, and this terrible sixth Earl — I thought you'd know what to do. If someone like you went to Richard — '

'Yes,' said Ruane. 'And told him what?'

I had been deluded again, self-deluded really, for I had worked out a scenario in my mind: Ruane, the ex-priest, would find some ritual to wipe out all trace of the hell-beast from Richard's mind. There would be a ceremony of purification, and here I had vague visions of solemn chanting, of the smoke of incense, and the gradual return of Richard to his own carefree self once more. It was another fantasy.

'Show him these!' I said bitterly, thrusting the sheaf of photocopies at Ruane.

He wouldn't take them. I let them fall.

'Consider this,' he said. 'You are dealing with experts. Don't you think that by now Richard knows all there is to know about his ancestor?'

'How?'

Ruane picked up the drawing of the tomb.

'Another catalyst,' he said. 'It will seem accidental to him, but he will have been guided to these early sources of legend and half-truths. I've no doubt that Richard Ulrome has studied all this material, and that he is eager to learn more about the evil at Monteine. Isn't that how it happened at the dinner-party? The guidance, I mean?'

He was right. Of course Richard would have been fed the information. They were more than clever enough to manipulate him.

'Then,' I said bitterly. 'I have to go to him myself.'

Ruane picked up the scattered papers. 'You will be killed.' He was so calm about it. 'Simon Miaolo is the source of the evil. He will not let you stand in his way. Now, what are they trying to do?'

'It all centres on the chapel on the cliffs,' I said slowly. 'At some time on the night of the last day of July. And on a legendary beast from the sea. I must have had a premonition of it when I saw the black fur on Richard. It's some kind of devil-worship.'

'Oh no,' he said. 'This is all about death.'

I'd heard someone else talk of death in that sombre manner. My financier friend had equated Miaolo with death.

'You see, Anne, this is to be a struggle for life, and there must be a death to complete the equation.'

Richard. I knew he was talking about Richard, but I was lost by now.

'Don't you see?' he asked. 'It's happened before. Four centuries ago, one of the Ulromes must have found out how to make contact with the ancient evil, the roaming husk that has haunted the Northern coasts since time immemorial.'

'A 'deadlie thing',' I quoted, and shuddered.

He took the rough-made cross and put my hand on it. 'Nothing can stand against this power.'

'I couldn't bear to lose Richard,' I said. 'They need him, don't they?'

'They do.' Ruane was frowning. 'But why? I have to know exactly what they need him for. And the answer isn't in these papers.'

I was going to say that they were all we had, but he hadn't finished his line of thought.

'Oh, there's enough in all the accounts to give an idea of the devilry at Monteine!' he exclaimed. 'But when all's truly considered, we have no more than our native wits could tell us. There's only one thing to be done. I have to go myself and see the chapel in the cliff.'

I made my mind up at once.

'We'll go now,' I said. 'I'll drive.'

Ruane got to his feet, surprisingly quickly. 'You'll not.'

'I'm not staying here!'

'You shall,' he said firmly. Before I could begin to argue, he said, 'Remember what the New York detective said. They won't allow you near him. Besides, this is for me to do alone. If you're seen around Monteine Castle in my company, there are bound to be questions.' He looked at himself in the mirror above the fireplace. 'We'd be an odd sight.'

'It's tomorrow night,' I said. 'I can't stand any more waiting. I know they've killed already so that Richard is the Monteine heir. I've got to get him away! What can we do?'

'Let me go,' he said. 'I promise I'll telephone within three hours of reaching Monteine. I'll ring on the hour, every hour, till you answer. If I need you, I'll ask you to come. In the meantime, go about your day as if you know nothing of this fearful matter. Please, Anne?'

He was right. It was quite possible that I was being watched, even now. It was better that I give them no cause for alarm. I had to put up with the agony of waiting.

'You'll need money — and my phone number. I'll write it down for you.'

I watched him cross the space in front of the park, a lonely, dishevelled but purposeful figure. I looked too for signs of watchers, but I saw none. For a few minutes, I was glad to be rid of Ruane. The stench of his clothes remained, so I opened some windows.

Two strong gins didn't begin to take the edge off the tension that was building up again. Nor did a phone call from Gloria do much to relieve my anxieties. Tony was in robust health. The antibiotics had done the trick, and he was feeling as if food had just been invented. He was staying the weekend, he decided.

When Gloria rang off, tension began to build again, until Richard rang an hour or so after Ruane left for Monteine. I had a wonderful vision of Richard at King's Cross asking me to come and pick him up. Another empty fantasy.

He was at the Castle, the weather was glorious — he didn't believe it was raining in London. Apparently he had been taken out that morning for a run in a new multi-hulled boat just up the coast from Monteine Landing. They'd had good winds and he was looking forward to taking us down to the South Coast within a few days to sort out the keel of his sea-boat. Wouldn't it be wonderful to take the boat out to the Bahamas? We could sail it, all of us together. He thought International might be willing to wait for two or three weeks before he took up the appointment.

I said it was all wonderful, just terrific. Then I said, without panic:

'Why don't you get on a train and come here, Richard? Tell them you've got a migraine. Or say the Duke of Edinburgh wants you to speak at one of those charity dinners. How about it, love?'

They'd be listening, but I went through every word I'd said. I sounded like any other selfish young woman whose man was away.

'I don't really think so, not now. But after the weekend without fail, Anne. I told you the Chairman's here, didn't I? Apparently, he's got one foot in the grave and it'll take all his energies up giving me the once-over and, hopefully, his blessing.'

'Oh, come on — get a train!' I said,

adding a few phrases of our own, very private. I didn't care who heard.

Richard sighed. 'Anne, if I could — '

'I need you, Richard!' I put as much passion into the plea as I could.

They were very clever then. A polite voice, a woman's cut in:

'I have your London call, sir. Will you take it now?'

Richard sounded politely puzzled and somewhat amused:

'I've been talking to the party in London for the last five minutes! Now, get off the line, there's a good girl!'

There was a series of harsh clicks, and a whining noise on the line. Through it, I heard Richard swearing. He promised to ring the next day if he could. Dimly, I also heard him say something about the interview.

He said goodbye.

They'd interrupted the call, of course. Every word had been monitored. Jensen and the others were probably listening to a tape of our conversation even now, minutes after it had finished.

I wanted Tony home then, but I

couldn't bear the thought of pitching him into the middle of the unresolved mystery I was going through. I would pass on my terrors to him.

The hours dragged. I could have left the flat at any time before about seven or eight at night — Ruane's train and bus connections couldn't have got him to Monteine before then, and there was the long walk along the cliff track to be accomplished and reversed; if, that is, he intended going to the chapel at all in the daylight, I cursed myself for a fool. I should have gone out, seen people, perhaps done my weekend shopping, or maybe I should have gone to see Tony.

I tried to ring Freda, but she wasn't at home. I chanced a call to her Bishopgate office, where they were cagey at first, but eventually said she'd gone away for a couple of days; there was a hint of envy in the coy answers that convinced me she'd gone weekending with Charkes Schofield.

I even thought of ringing Bill Marr. He'd helped me, but I was reluctant to inflict my misery on him at this time. I wished then that I'd had parents to rely on, but how could I explain to those sad old bigoted people that my lover was in peril from a grim-faced man who was in league with Satan?

I was alone.

There was enough gin in the flat to make me bemused. I was in a shocking state by nine o'clock, and I was staring at the phone as if it were alive. I stopped drinking when I realized how bad I was.

I watched television after that, right through to eleven, half dozing, then jerked erect as I heard the jangle of the telephone bell.

I fumbled with the receiver and heard Ruane saying hello, was this Anne Blackwell?

'What's happened? Have you seen him? Did you go to the chapel? Ruane, I don't think I can stand it any longer!'

'Get a hold of yourself! Anne, for the love of God try to keep your sanity! Now, what are you doing? Is there no one with you?'

'Everyone's away — I've no one! Have you seen him?'

'No, but I'll get along the cliffs tonight

— there's enough moon to see by, and I've used some of your money to buy a strong torch. I called you to tell you what I'm doing, and to make sure you stay put and don't try anything foolish. Try to sleep, you need it! Just let me do this, and I'll call you tomorrow morning. Now, do you want to hear what I've found?'

With the shrewdness of the near-drunk, I said:

'You haven't been drinking, have you?'

He wasn't shocked. 'I have,' he said. 'Only so I could talk to the locals in the pub. I talked to some of the older men who still know the old legends. They haven't got it quite the same as the text you showed me, but they remember the evil from the sea. 'From the sea-road', that's how they put it. 'Along the sea-road at Lammas-tide'. I'll know what must be done some time tomorrow. You were right about the aura of the place. It stinks of evil. The villagers sense it too, but they think they're uneasy because of the strangers at the Castle. That's all I have time for — I'll watch at the chapel for your man. Now, will you try to rest?'

I said I would, then I told him how Richard's call had been interrupted; he didn't seem surprised.

I said I'd thought of sneaking out of the flat and driving to meet him but he wouldn't hear of it. He wanted to see the chapel that night. I asked for his phone number and an address where I could contact him, expecting him to name a guesthouse or a hotel. He said he'd been offered a bed by one of the villagers who had taken him to be a down-and-out: there was no telephone. I realized that he couldn't approach a hotel or a guest-house, not in his dishevelled condition.

He had shown considerable shrewd-ness, I realized; optimism flooded me as he rang off. Ruane was to call me in the morning, at ten, then at eleven, and so on, until I answered.

He sounded unworried, even when I'd asked him exactly what he thought would happen at the chapel on Lammas' Eve.

'Something worse than you could possibly imagine,' he had said, in a harsh tone. 'Evil that's as old as mankind, maybe older. But nothing that cannot be overcome by a resolute spirit and the assistance of Jesus Christ and His Holy Saints.'

I remembered the tortured strength in the figure on the Cross, and I began to believe that Ruane could ward off the evil from the sea. I did as Ruane had told me and tried to sleep.

I slept in fitful spasms. In clearer moments I had moments of insight into my experiences at Monteine: there was one frightful vision of myself in the moonlight on the cliffs at Monteine. A head turned towards me saying something I couldn't hear for the crash of the unseen waves on the black rocks far below.

It was Simon Miaolo.

And the head was stone.

My dreams were more dreadful than any so far.

17

I knew I had slept late. My exhaustion had finally caught up with me and I couldn't struggle out of the hours-long sequence of nightmarish dreams, even though I knew that I should be awake and alert. I finally awoke to see the grey light of a miserably wet day reflected on the grey slate roofs beyond the park. I kept perfectly still as if hiding.

I didn't want to face the day. It was Lammas Eve. I stumbled across to the clock on the dressing table. It said three minutes to eleven, so of course I didn't believe it. I looked at my watch, which was on my wrist all the time. The time was confirmed: I'd missed Ruane's call.

I must have slept right through the strident shrilling of the bell. But I couldn't have! I was badly hungover, but I could work out that Ruane hadn't called at ten o'clock as he had promised.

Then I thought of making tea; but I

made sure that the phones in the bedroom and in the lounge were set firmly on their cradles first.

I watched that phone for two more hours. Time dragged. I washed my hair, got myself presentable, cooked a meal and threw most of it away, but all that only took half an hour.

At one he didn't ring. Soon afterwards there was a caller who wanted someone called Mark. Wrong number I told her, and cut her off before she could argue. Then there were three calls in quick succession, two of them trivial bits of business matters, the third one Bill Marr.

I told him I was very grateful for his researching, and that he'd have to come and see us after the wedding. Then I started weeping and I had to say I'd got a cold and wasn't in the mood to talk. He sounded puzzled, but he wished Richard and me well. I wouldn't let him talk about the legend, nor indeed about any of the Ulromes, Richard included.

I read all the document again, trying to fit it all into place. Richard was the link between the terrible old man Simon

Miaolo and the thing that would swim along the white moon-road to the chapel. Miaolo was an expert in death. His words came back stronger than ever, for I had a rare gift of memory:

'Make no mistakes. My patience is unlimited, but my time becomes less. Success is what I promised myself. If there is anything — anything — that should be done, name it. You will be failing in your duty if you keep back any circumstance that affects the outcome of the Monteine operation. Remember this. If for one moment, on one occasion, some proof of the existence of that power or force we seek can be achieved — once! — however vague, however insubstantial, however indefinite: only so much proof as will make the slightest crack in my lifelong agnosticism, then you will have your promised rewards, and I mine!'

That was what he had said. His face had been contorted with longing as he flayed his hearers into ruthless action. The intensity of his lust for a glimpse of the supernatural had terrified me. Its memory drove me to a horrified panic.

Ruane hadn't called me, and it was past three o'clock. I could see Miaolo's face etched on my mind with acid. I could see the smooth deadliness of Kresak too; a series of those deadly men and women at Monteine Castle began to bewilder me, so that I fell into a trance-like state.

I could see the alert, greedy faces in a ring, with great white-gold stars glittering in a velvet sky, not one I had seen before. Inside the ring, the earth was turned back, and there were movements of a clay-caked figure. I was watching some kind of terrible ritual, I knew.

I had an utter conviction that I had experienced again an insight into matters beyond my comprehension, certainly beyond my knowledge, just as I had seen a terrible presence when we were in the beautiful, deadly tower room, just as the line of black for had been a premonition of evil.

What Miaolo was so desperately seeking was near, very near.

I knew that the fearful, atavistic *thing* that had left men torn so many summers ago was at hand, waiting for a summons.

Ruane had said so much over the phone. The 'deadlie thing' was near.

Richard would have to call on the beast from the sea. And when he called, he would die. Beyond that I could not go. My moment of fearful insight was over. I got to my feet. It was to be tonight. And I was waiting for an alcoholic ex-priest to call me.

I didn't feel any hatred of Ruane. That part of me was long gone. It was plain enough what I should do.

I had to go to the Castle and take my chances against whoever stood between me and Richard.

Before leaving, I left a note for Gloria explaining that she was to contact Freda Langdon in the event of my non-return.

I didn't feel brave. I don't quite know what I felt. But, at three-thirty, I walked out to my little Fiat, avoided talking to a garrulous young woman neighbour, and pointed the car North.

It was at least a six-hour drive to the coast, and then there was the winding drive to the cliffs. I should make it by ten or so that evening.

I listened to the radio for hours. Traffic built up on the approaches to the motorway, and there was a solid stream of vehicles moving at sixty to seventy miles an hour, for mile after mile. I got out of the rain-belt near Watford Gap. There was an even heavier concentration of vehicles.

I was about ten miles South of York when I came to a long, slow line of single traffic. *Road repairs*. I could have avoided it if only I'd listened to the road reports on the radio, but I had tuned in to a music station to keep myself awake. As it was, we crawled at fifteen miles an hour, and the sun vanished behind banks of trees. It had taken me longer than I'd expected to get that far North. I hadn't stopped, not once.

Time was passing fast. I needed coffee and a rest. I was in that stupefied state which comes about eighteen hours after a lot of alcohol. So I got careless.

I hit one of those metal cones they use to mark off lanes, not too hard, and I thought I'd done no damage until I got clear of the roadworks and the steering started to go soft as I picked up to thirty.

It got worse as I accelerated to get to the Fiat's comfortable cruising speed, then I found the car sliding towards the side of the road. A tyre had gone, but I didn't know it.

I was lucky, for the truck-driver behind me saw what was happening well before I did. He was hooting, braking, flashing his lights and generally acting as a warning to the rest of the traffic. So he didn't plough into me, and he'd already moved out so no one could overtake him and thus cause a series of accidents when I swung out of control. I was going uphill too, another piece of good fortune,

I didn't see it that way. It was five hours since I had left my flat: there was so little time left.

The truck-driver saw my shocked face and produced a flask of tea. He looked at the tyre whilst I tried to stop shaking, then he asked about the spare.

He said he'd soon put it on for me and I wasn't to worry.

That was when a police-car stopped.

I suppose it wasn't too much of a coincidence that it turned out to be manned by the same crew that had stopped me a week before. I got the same kindly treatment.

'Getting to know one another, aren't we, Miss,' the fat sergeant said. I thought he'd have long forgotten me. He was watching me closely, though he didn't appear to be doing so. He'd be thinking of breathalysing me. 'It is your car, isn't it, Miss?'

We went through the gambits, so that I had to give fairly complicated answers about the reason for the tyre giving out. My answers were coherent; they seemed to satisfy him.

'Look at the spare, Miss,' said the truck-driver. 'I'm sorry, it won't do.'

I looked and saw at once that the spare tyre was old and worn.

'It was a new tyre!' I said, incredulously. 'It came new with the car — I bought it only a few months ago!'

The sergeant had a look. So did his constable.

'It's a bald tyre, Miss,' the sergeant said.

'Won't it get me to the coast?' I said. 'I've got to go now. Now!'

The sergeant shook his head. 'Illegal, Miss.' Richard was about eighty miles away, more than two hours of careful driving. My car was useless.

'Sorry, Miss,' said the truck driver, who was getting uneasy about the presence of the policemen. 'It's asking for trouble driving on worn tyres. You know what's happened, don't you? You've been done by someone at your garage. Someone's nicked your spare and left you this rubbish. Right?' he asked the policemen.

They agreed. 'You don't have a lot of luck in Yorkshire, do you, love?' said the constable.

I didn't realize that I was weeping until the sergeant began coughing. 'Now then, love, it's not so bad. All you need is a tyre. Up the road there's a tyre specialist. We're going that way now.' He put the spare in the police vehicle.

The truck-driver winked and grinned at me. He thought I was pulling the old feminine trick. He looked disappointed when I didn't wink back.

'I really have to get there tonight,' I said morosely.

The truck-driver roared away; we followed in the police-car, for they insisted I needed a cup of coffee whilst the tyre was changed. Very gently and with a subtlety I hadn't thought to find in such men, they asked, why I was in such a depressed state. I said I was visiting someone who was in trouble, and I gratefully took up their suggestion that the someone I was visiting was ill.

I kept quiet after that. The sun was down when we got back to the Fiat. They'd been quick, efficient and obliging at the tyre station.

'Not too fast,' warned the sergeant, when the constable had changed the wheel again. 'Get a new spare first thing tomorrow, Miss, that's what you should do.'

I said I would.

No one was to blame for the delay except the greedy thief at my garage. I hoped he'd crash on my stolen tyre. But whoever he was he was only a link in the long chain of circumstances which delayed me on my final journey to Monteine. Charles Schofield was the first, with his urbane confidence. It had led to hope, then despair, and not only once. I had come to trust the shambling hulk Ruane, with his odd diffident strength that had failed me. I had waited for a bitter night, then another interminable morning for him to call and I had come to the realization that I was going to the Castle. Neither Kresak nor the whole insidious gang of them would prevent me from reaching Richard if I could arrive boldly in daylight; I convinced myself that they would not dare to harm me, not when there might be witnesses about, not in broad daylight, with the trippers filling the lanes, and walkers by the dozen along the cliff-top path.

Now, the light was fading and it would be another two hours before I got to the coast. As if to provide a further warning, thick black thunderclouds blotted out the last of the dim sunlight as I drove northwest towards the sea The light car was pushed hard to the off-side by sudden gusts. Then the rain began, great starred splashes on the windscreen followed by a hard-driven downpour.

The effort of concentrating on the road kept me awake. I had to grip the wheel hard and peer out to catch sight of bends and road-signs in the winding lanes that led over the bare moorland.

My first glimpse of the sea dismayed me, then suddenly the early lights of Monteine Landing glittered ahead. Beyond the tiny harbour I caught a glimpse of great waves briefly white-capped in the flash of sheet lightning. I felt my hands shaking on the wheel.

I had to drive up to the Castle, I told myself. That, and demand entrance. I calmed for a few moments when a shelf of rock hid the sea's frantic commotion.

They would be waiting.

I thought of the rocks. There was a track quite easily negotiable by cars running from the Castle to the cliff-top. I could see myself slumped over the wheel and Kresak carefully guiding the car towards the edge. They would kill me.

I made myself drive on.

Despite my fear I stopped at the place where I had parked the car on my last visit to Monteine Castle. I switched the engine off. The rain drummed unceasingly on the thin metal. I couldn't see a thing through the windows.

For no reason I can explain now, I had to get out of the car. And, once out, I had to move towards the Castle. Terror can do that. I knew how the mouse can actually look around for the cat that will kill it. After the long session of torture, it has to recognize that the end is inevitable. I had to see the end of it all.

I looked at my watch. It was ten minutes to eleven.

My movements were quite automatic. I don't remember fastening my coat securely or jamming the plastic hat on my head, or changing from my driving shoes, or finding the heavy-duty torch on the tray. I walked, head-down towards the Castle in a wind-buffeted, cold, dour, rain-lashed and completely terrified daze.

When a sudden coruscation of lightning showed me the whole of the landscape — Castle, cliff-top, thunderous, towering waves, and trees half bent in the gale's fury — I didn't particularly respond: I accepted the colossal release of energy as a useful illumination of the cliff path.

I wasn't going to the Castle, of course. It was Lammas Eve, so there was no point in going to the Castle.

Richard would not be in his bed. The Earl of Monteine had other duties.

I used my torch carefully, shielding it from the North tower where I was sure there would be watchers even on such a night. The force of the wind increased as I neared the Cliff's edge, but I was in no danger for my ankle was quite better; I had walking shoes on; I was able negotiate the rocky part of the track which had given me so much trouble after the dinner party.

It took me about fifteen minutes to reach the cleft where the chapel lay. I used the torch carefully and only when I needed it. I didn't want to alert any of the sadistic gang. I couldn't see very much, so I waited for the lightning to show me the way.

It filled the horizon seawards, dazzling with a blue-white radiance of supernatural beauty. What little night vision I had went in that instant, so I lost my bearings and went off the track. I stumbled over a rock and felt the rain slashing at my face. I didn't know which way to go to find the track. I could be on the edge of the cliff. I dropped the torch in my fright.

I heard the sea's growling thunder at the foot of the cliffs. I looked hard, but saw only blackness: one more step might take me over the edge, and I could be drifting downwards, my hands clawing at the invisible rain for support, and the fanged black rocks waiting below.

I panicked and moved slightly. I screamed, but it kept me rooted to the spot and I managed to force myself to think of Richard and his peril.

I knelt quickly, once I recovered. I scrabbled amongst the stinging nettles, the loose rock and the mossy grass. And then, in a brief moment of pure ecstasy, my hand fell on the slimy rubber of the torch.

I got to my feet, swaying with relief. Momentarily, the wind dropped. Another of those colossal lightning flashes shot across the sea. I was a yard from the edge of the cliff.

I turned towards the land.

I saw a shape moving close towards me. Huge. A huge formless shape. I stepped back, gagging with pure terror; I knew it for a deadly thing. I knew it for the beast.

Monstrous arms reached for me. I couldn't scream, and as I was seized I felt myself fall. I could face no more.

18

I learned afterwards that I was unconscious for only a few seconds. It seemed much more. I was aware that I was being dragged, and that someone was saying, over and over again, 'Don't scream, for the love of Jesus God, don't scream again, just keep quiet!'

It sounded like gibberish the first time, but eventually I knew that Ruane was talking to me.

'Jesus God! Couldn't you stay away? Couldn't you let it be for the night?'

'Ruane!'

'So it is, but keep quiet, they're down there!'

My night vision returned and I could make out his features. He wore some kind of tarpaulin raincoat, a formless dull-gleaming garment; it was no wonder that I had taken him for the thing of the legend.

'You didn't call!' I gasped. 'Where's

Richard? Have you seen him? What happened, Ruane, you didn't call!'

'I've had things to do — they took me all the morning, then when I got to a public phone, it was broken. I tried to telephone later from another phone box but you weren't answering. Now get a hold of yourself! There's devilry here and more to come. I was watching the chapel when I saw you lose your torch so I had to make sure you didn't fall over the cliff.'

We were out of the worst of the storm; I remembered then a small shelf of rock in the hill. Ruane had half-dragged, half-carried me about a dozen yards from the cliff path. I felt the slow burn of the nettle stings and the sharp pain of scratches on my legs and arms. It didn't matter that Ruane hadn't been able to ring me, not now.

'Is Richard safe?'

He hesitated. 'He is down there with the others.'

I began to move.

'*No!*' Ruane said harshly. 'Leave be, woman! Listen to me!'

The grip on my arm was too strong. I

still felt weak from the blacking-out.

'Are you calm?'

'Yes,' I said. 'Now, let me go!'

'Not yet, woman — not till just before midnight. We can do nothing till the moon is bright!'

The rain found us in our shelter; I gasped at its stinging power. Lightning, followed almost at once by thunder, left my senses reeling.

'I have to go to him down there,' I sobbed.

'Not yet! Wait for the moonlight — the deadly thing rides the moon's back, and that is when we can strike!'

'Have you seen Richard?' I grated.

'Yes. A few minutes ago. And five others, one a woman.'

'They'll kill him — you said so: you said death and life go together!'

'And still we must wait, because they'll kill us both if we go now! But just wait till the deadly one comes from the sea, and then we have a chance! I saw last night how it could be done, Anne!'

'Where?'

'At the chapel, Anne, I saw the evil thing, the worst of all!'

'What did you see? Tell me!'

'Very well,' Ruane said. 'I watched and waited last night, and an hour before midnight I saw them come. A young man, and three others. One was old but he was still active. This was the evil one, he had the true stench of evil, though the others had no compassion in their souls. Your man was far away, his spirit barely within his body, for they had worked on him one of the smaller mysteries of the occult. I saw his eyes when he looked out to the black sea and back to the chapel. Anne, he was calling on something the very thought of which shakes and chills me worse than any frozen ice.'

Ruane's breathing was shallow and fast and he radiated that too-familiar aura of terror. I knew it well.

'Calling on what?'

'The tomb in the photograph. It was open.'

Lightning flashed, the wind howled m a peculiarly vicious fashion. I barely noticed any of it.

'A ritual,' he said. 'A ceremony of invocation. But one I have no knowledge of, though the words are the same old evil.'

'And?'

'They waited for an hour, your man watching by the tomb. Then something moved.'

We waited, each wrapped in a bitter horror. I think that Ruane relied on me then for strength. There was so much anguish in his tone when he spoke of the scene in the chapel, that I am sure he had used up what for want of a better expression could be called his spiritual energy.

'The tomb,' I said. 'A movement? What?'

'An arm pointed at Richard Ulrome. The fair young man.'

'I'm going to him!' I kicked out and felt my heavy shoe drive into his side.

He grunted, but retained his strong grip on my arm.

'Don't, Anne,' he said. 'Wait for the moonlight!'

'And what then?' I yelled back.

'Destroy the beast,' he said in a low but stronger voice.

I let my arm drop. 'The beast?'

'The deadly thing! Oh, it will come, for

Richard Ulrome will call it — he will have the power.'

'God in Heaven,' I whispered.

'Evil can be wiped out,' he said fiercely. 'There are the wandering husks of devils that wait beyond the shades of night for misguided creatures like those in the chapel, but they can be confounded. But you must wait, Anne. They'll hear you — they're watchful, They take no chances. Simon Miaolo wants his life to last forever, so why should he not be cautious to the last?'

I had known what the experiment or conjuration was all along, and I had only recently allowed the pieces to fall together into a mental pattern; I still could not accept the solution.

'How could his life last forever?'

'Evil is undying, Anne. He will become a part of it.'

'How?'

'Blood will have blood. Woman, know this. We are to see the most terrible of the manifestations of evil. We are in the presence of death, and we must endure even worse.'

'There is worse, Ruane?'

Could it be?

His deep, sure brogue rang like a gong sounding around the place of ancient burial. There was an assured authority in Ruane now.

'Believe it, Anne. The beast has been called from the sea. It has been summoned to give life. It will demand a requital.'

Blood.

Evil, death and blood. I heard myself shouting,

'Blood? Blood! Is that what you say? Whose blood?'

I knew. Richard was to be the sacrifice. Miaolo would be one of the undying.

'You can — you will — you must use your powers, Ruane! Will they be strong enough?'

'That's to be seen.'

'But what can we do — you said it can be destroyed! How?'

Ruane got to his feet. 'It can. And will be — by the oldest way of all, the sure way!'

I felt danger, fear and a sudden blazing

of energy. 'Tell me what you're planning, Ruane. I can't wait again, not any more. Tell me!'

Ruane released my arm. 'If I tell you what I learned here, will you wait?'

The sky was still overcast, but I could see a pale light behind higher clouds. The wind still screamed over the sheltered cleft where we stood, but the storm was blowing itself out. The moonlight was hidden by a thin curtain of cloud. Soon it would pour down on the black sea.

'If you can stop them, then tell me.'

He did so, in a very few words. The seamen of Monteine Landing recognized his strange aura of power. They told him their own garbled version of the legends and offered him shelter for the night. Later, they found the things that he would need, all without asking for an explanation. They knew what Lammas Eve could mean.

I listened in horror and disbelief. A brief vision of my son's sleeping face came to me, and then Ruane's voice sounded as clear as a bell.

'Steel and fire! The old way!'

In the increasing light, he showed me the worn shaft and the dull-gleaming blade of an axe. I shuddered. There was more: he had with him the crucifix and a package rather more than a foot long and a few inches wide.

It didn't seem necessary to ask any more questions.

19

Out across the North Sea the moonlight filtered stronger and stronger through high, dense clouds. I looked up once and fancied that I saw the moon half-obscured in such a way that it gave a fleeting impression of a death's head; I looked back at the sea. There was a distinct pale moonlit road on the black sea. Ruane stopped me as we reached the overgrown private track that led to the ruined chapel.

I could see a white-yellow glimmer from the porch.

'You'll wait — be sure, Anne! Will you?'

'Yes.'

'Take these.' I was to help. 'It's the Fire. Open the packet.'

I was fiercely impatient now. 'It's near midnight,' I said. But I wanted to know about Ruane's 'fire'. There were two cardboard tubes, each one well waxed. My hands were shaking.

'Here,' said Ruane, and his movements were quick and certain. He took the tubes and quickly and deftly removed the wax windings. 'They're old, but they're m good condition. They burn well.'

He said it grimly and with satisfaction. *Ruane's fire.*

This was what he meant when he had said that the local fishermen had supplied him with what he needed: they were flares — distress signals. I'd seen Richard light one to test a pack; the heat and light they produced was tremendous.

'Pull the cord,' he said. 'It lights the flare. When I say.'

I looked at Ruane's face and saw that exposure, lack of food and deadly tension had sharpened his coarse features. His head was hunched forward from heavy shoulders; the axe rested easily in one great hand. In the other, he gripped the crucifix. He radiated a divine power. Ahead I made out moving shadows against the steady light from the oil lamp.

'Follow quietly!' he whispered hoarsely.

The wind howled suddenly, far louder than before. A rushing fury of force pushed me and I reeled helplessly. Ruane grunted, himself driven away from the path. And then, with the same lack of warning, all noise stopped abruptly.

It was so sudden that I caught my breath and cut off the protesting gasp that should have followed my near-fall. In the space of a half-second, the night was calm, utterly still, and bitterly cold.

I felt myself numbed by disbelief for a moment; and then the fear came. The moon was a great beacon in the night-sky, untouched now by cloud. I shuddered and thought of my appalling dreams of the night before. The moon had been bright, brighter than this, though the sense of terror was the same.

I heard Ruane bite back his breath also. We were waiting. The time had come. I caught myself murmuring 'The deadlie thing — ' and I heard the call.

It began low, a lost and wailing sound, but there was nothing pitiful about it; though the volume was slight there was an eerie menace in that far-off cry that brought a cold sweat of terror, and caused Ruane to hold the high carven cross up to the glittering, deadly moonlight.

'Run!' he told me. 'To the chapel!'

I did not need a second reminder. I could visualize the wide track of the white moonlight and the phantasmagorical shape gliding fast towards the shore. What I had seen in the stone and conjured up in the tower room was here again, announcing its coming with a ghoulish cry that echoed and re-echoed across the white sea-lane and the bleak rocks. This was no dream, no passing fancy. Ruane's warning was harsh, his tone brooked no argument.

I followed his ungainly progress, There was no alternative but to run towards the chapel. On either side, the slopes were almost precipitous. We had to run for the shelter of the mausoleum of the Earls of Monteine. Behind us, I heard the indescribably terrifying call of the thing from the sea. It had a lost, haunting, yet menacing quality that brought back every terrifying vision of childhood dreams sharp and fresh.

I thought of the open tomb ahead, and the hand raised after four hundred-odd years of stillness. 'Ruane!' I gasped.

We were at the fallen rocks and the demolished masonry.

'Quiet!' he whispered hoarsely, his breathing ragged. 'Through here — this side chapel.'

Ruane, for all his bulk, moved silently down a passageway to the right of the crypt. We could hide there, I saw at once.

I looked in and stood for a moment. I saw Richard between two lanterns. His back was to me. He faced the tomb, and it was as Ruane had said: the lid of the great carven tomb had been removed. I could see three of those present, apart from Richard: Kresak, dimly seen beyond the tomb; Fitch, shrunken and nervous, staring out at the dark, and, huddled in a wheelchair, a gaunt straining figure, mouth open and eyes glittering. It was Miaolo, the man who was in league with death, the fabulously wealthy man who had enticed Richard to this place of horrors.

Ruane did not let me stay. He pushed me. The handle of the axe caught me solidly in the ribs. I nearly yelled out with shock, but his low whisper cautioned me again: 'On his life!' he whispered furiously.

I realized that I had two fingers looped through the pull-string of the flare. I had seen my enemy,

Ruane jabbed me again, but I was already moving. We were to hide, I knew that. We ducked under barely-seen arches. Ruane had been there before, it was obvious he knew the place. He scrabbled quietly to avoid fallen masonry, and then we were swallowed up by the darkness; parts of the wall between the side-chapel and crypt had fallen in, but here we were in solid rock tunnelled hundreds of years before. The ground was cold and wet.

Ruane slithered forward; I followed and then we turned sharp right. The steady light of the oil lamps was ahead. I could not see into the chapel, but I heard the voices.

Miaolo's was the strongest, though I identified those of Fitch and the Sievel woman. So they're all gathered, I thought fleetingly. To greet the living death from the sea.

Miaolo called again, dominating the hubbub:

'Kresak, be ready to lift me!'

A wave of bitter cold washed down the tunnel towards us. With it came a stench I recognized. I had sensed it before, by that uncanny premonition of mine, foetid, horrible, saline, the product of centuries' decay. My thoughts were a weird confusion of images, but the dominant one was of the sea — the rolling, black sea and the track of a monstrous primeval force leaving a glittering track in the moonlight. All life came from the sea: this was the return of something older than any form of life known to us: it was the undeniable stench of primordial evil.

Ruane whispered harsh reminders to be silent, to be cautious as we went on.

He pushed on, and I followed. There was more light now.

The side-chapel was walled with the sarcophagi of later Ulromes. I could see, in the dim light from the mausoleum proper, the rectangular blocks of stone behind which lay the lords and ladies of Monteine. One slab of stone had cracked, and I could fancy that I saw the yellow bones of long-dead noblemen; fact and fancy were inextricably mixed. I gripped hard on the waxed tubes to ascertain whether I was in nightmare or in the grimmest of realities.

Kresak's voice resolved it for me, for just as we reached the mausoleum proper his voice rang out in that accentless English:

'My Lord Earl, you must summon your visitor once more!'

There was a deferential yet authoritative quality in the voice, and a barely discernible tremor of fear. I might have called out to Richard, but Ruane had me in a tight grip. He let me loose when I was still.

I wriggled sideways and saw what he had already seen.

There was a small area around the tomb of the sixth Earl, which was lit by the two oil lamps. Beyond, all was shadow. We were hidden by fallen rocks and the debris of a wall of shattered tombs, None of the intent, scared circle of watchers could have seen us, had they been able to spare a thought for intruders at that strange and macabre scene.

Miaolo's fists were clenched tight against his thin chest. The Sievel woman was pressed back against a small dais where an altar might have once stood. She had the look of a woman terrified beyond belief. Fitch was in the same case. His whole demeanour suggested that of a man at the end of his resources. But Jensen was standing upright, a slight incredulous smile on his face. Of them all, perhaps only he and Miaolo looked unafraid. Jensen had the scholar's nerveless temerity; Miaolo believed he would not die. Kresak had the fanatical air of a man determined to stand against all that could possibly occur but he was bitterly afraid too.

As for Richard, he gazed calmly across the open tomb of his ancestor with no appearance of anything but a mild boredom. I knew the look. I have seen the eyes of those under heavy doses of drugs many times. Richard was totally under the control of the creatures around him. He would do what they told him to do.

'My Lord Earl,' said Kresak sharply. 'You know the words. Call on the visitor!'

His face was set in vicious lines, his voice had the lash of steel. Miaolo tensed, ready to speak again; it was unnecessary, for Richard turned towards the tunnel entrance. I heard him call out loud and clearly, but in words that had no meaning for me. Their cadences were guttural, the individual sounds like those of beasts.

The cry in answer came almost as he finished. It rang out from the cliff tops, filling the silence with its horrific menace. There was loneliness and terror in the cry and a great baying hatred. I thought of Ruane's words and saw in a moment of psychic truth, that the thing, whatever it was could realize itself only through the agency of those it hated most, the human kind. It needed life to make it live. Life blood, death. That was in its call and its terrible threat.

Richard was smiling. I saw the smile he had worn when I had watched him, unseen, on another night. There was a hint of evil in that smile, for the lips were drawn finely back revealing his whit teeth; and emphasizing the high cheek-bones, which stood out white and stark in his thin face. The menace from the sea found an equal response in him.

Miaolo was furiously excited. His voice was high-pitched, yet still the most commanding, more vicious than Kre-sak's, and almost as frightening in its intensity as the call from the cliffs.

'Don't move — anybody — !' he cried. 'I must see the demon — see it, watch it live! It must have blood so I live again!'

Richard ignored him. He was watching the ruined porch way. I had the feeling that he was utterly lost to me. Ruane stopped me from pushing the stiff cord of the flare so that I could burn the panting, growling figure in the wheelchair. I wanted Miaolo dead. 'Still!' whispered Ruane, as again a wild, uncanny howling came from near the entrance to the chapel.

The stench of evil was stronger. Even as I watched, I saw the effects of the drop in temperature. The inside of the chapel with a pearly mist as droplets of solidified. There was the smell

tissue and knots of blood-vessels writhed beneath a gleaming, scaly surface. The head was a ferocious mask — I try not to see it in my dreams, but it comes back: snarling, fangs gleaming, and cunning red eyes ablaze; but there was anguish and brute power and undying hatred too. All about that ghastly form was the reek of decay and the stench of evil, I could see at once where all the stories of ravening sea-beasts came from; one such thing loose on a coast would remain in folk-memory for ever, changing as the language changed and as its appearances became more and more infrequent. This was the atavistic form of evil, older than man, maybe not from our Earth at all.

It wasn't enormous in size. But it had about it the mysterious evil that we all fear. I told myself I couldn't open my eyes again; yet I did, for I knew that the ghoulish thing was nearing Richard. I heard its wet steps nearing him. So I found the courage and looked.

I had thought that nothing could be worse, yet what I saw was worse. It added an extra dimension of pure horror, for the dead had returned to life.

There was movement in the tomb.

Miaolo was upright, eyes shining in wonder. Kresak was down. Jensen had his hands before his face. Ruane was gabbling prayers: only Miaolo and I could watch as the long-dead sixth Earl of Monteine played his part in the frightful scene.

The oil lamps were shrouded by the dank white mist which filled the mausoleum, yet I could see the great stone tomb and the rearing, skeletal figure rising from its depths; I could see, too, the grimacing skull, still with remnants of leathery flesh and thin threads of grey-white hair; and there were noises from the tomb, as more evidence of a kind of life in that frightful miasmic mist.

Where terror had taken over during the earlier part of the evening, I was now saved from going into a trance by a furious revulsion; I loathed the grimacing corpse and the monster it had summoned. I screamed and dragged my arm from Ruane's numbing grip.

He had become rigid with shock; I had

to act, he didn't try to stop me. The corpse ground out a rasping coughing incantation to the shadowy presence at the chapel entrance.

I scrabbled for the stout cord of the flares as the skeletal hand reached out towards Richard — whether in some kind of satanic benediction, or whether threateningly I did not know, nor do I know now — and I screamed to Richard to beware. No one heard or saw. Except Ruane.

'Not yet!' he grated. 'It does not live — nor will, woman! The living dead takes part in the ritual — it must be destroyed, but it is not the worst we shall see tonight! Watch!'

The corpse was fully upright. The long-dead Earl's arms were beckoning to the impatient snuffling beast. Miaolo gasped and, with a supreme effort, got to his feet. He took a feeble step forward, his face alight with triumph.

'Soon!' Ruane cried, and Miaolo darted a quick glance towards the back of the chapel where we were hidden. 'Anne, the flares! The beast from the sea demands blood for blood. It will have a new life for the old.'

My unspoken and unformulated questions coalesced around these tendrils of arcane knowledge. The remains of the Sixth Earl had moved. That was enough of sheer uncomprehending horror for the moment: what that had to do with Richard, I could not discern.

I had to trust Ruane,

Old, worn, and at times incoherent he might be; but now he radiated power.

This was the Old Church pitted against the primeval evil.

The Evil at Monteine.

The thing had recognized Richard. There was an alertness about the ghastly beast that signified intelligence. It knew that there was to be an affinity between itself and the new Earl of Monteine. A pact was to be renewed.

The corpse groaned through a decayed larynx, breath from empty lungs, breath full of the dust of four hundred years, yet with a fearful authority. Not words, but recognizably a command.

'Flares!' said Ruane.

I fumbled with the cord. It slipped from my grasp for my fingers were enfeebled by the biting cold. Ruane yelled at me again. He pleaded with me. The words made no sense,

I was far gone with terror at my failure to help Richard. 'It has to be before the metamorphosis!' Ruane bawled, but I could make nothing of the word.

Ruane gave me up. He leapt forward, fell heavily, recovered himself and ran towards the tomb. He did not look at the ferocious beast, which had advanced a little into the entrance of the chapel. Axe high, Ruane's purpose was clear. He would strike with all his strength at the beckoning, rasping corpse.

He would remove the conduit to Richard that was the deadly inheritance of his line. I had a moment's mad comprehension of what he was to do. He would, in a sense, disconnect the line, the conduit, the channel of life-force that ran directly down the years, from Richard's evil and grotesque ancestor to his own marvellously dependable and utterly honourable self. My man might be alone. But he could be saved. I would do what I had to do.

'Ruane!' I screamed.

Kresak recognized a human danger, and he could act, He had little need to exert himself. A skilful kick brought Ruane down. There was a long low wailing noise from the beast and I expected it to spring. It didn't, and my nerve came back.

Still with numbed fingers, I ripped out the cord. Ruane had told me what to do. On no account must I look at the flare. It would dazzle me, and I should be blinded for minutes. I was to hold it away from me, and shield its radiance with my body. I did exactly as he had said.

I ran awkwardly past the slumped form of Ruane, who had his hands before his face as a guard against the rushing light, past Kresak who, even though part-blinded, tried to stop me, and towards the great open tomb. I stopped three or four yards away, for I had not conquered my terror. But I saw Richard's handsome, evil face and I hated with all the strength of my soul: I could hate, strike, destroy I threw the spitting, rushing flare straight at the rotting corpse of the sixth Earl of Monteine.

Sparks showered white-hot on a winding sheet that caught fire at once. The flare bounced against the side of the tomb and fell onto the straining undead figure. Immediately flames burst from the sarcophagus in a blinding sheet, blue and green flame shot with gold and red. There must have been more unguent-soaked winding-sheets, for the heat from the tomb began to disperse the dank mist. Kresak recovered fast.

I saw him rushing at me, and I couldn't avoid the blow. His fist caught me on the side of the cheek, breaking the thin bone. I hardly felt it. Ruane was on his knees, calling out something. I saw Richard staring at the beast. I tried to get up, but I was in shock, so I saw much of what happened on my knees.

Ruane, catching up the axe, then knocked down again by Kresak; Miaolo beating at the corpse with his bare hands trying to douse the flames. The corpse, seemingly undisturbed by the gouting fires, mouthing terrible rasping phrases even as the heat charred the bones of its skull. *And Richard*. He was walking towards the beast.

'Richard, if you love me!' I screamed. 'Stop!'

Miaolo was yelling in Italian.

Kresak looked about him, undecided, bewildered. He listened to Miaolo's furious gabbling and yelled back. Jensen joined in, but I couldn't make out what he was saying. Then Ruane stumbled away from the fire and from Kresak's fists. I thought for a moment that he was trying to escape but I was wrong.

He staggered momentarily and then moved very fast towards the hiding-place from which we had watched the commencement of those terrible events, and, in one quick movement, he had snatched up the crucifix and hurled it the length of the chapel with great strength and certain aim.

I watched its flight. In the shooting flames from the tomb, I saw the strained face of the blind man's Christ, and there were grace and power in the carven features. In a long parabola it travelled, until it was swallowed up by the darkness where the beast and its frightful miasmic aura waited for Richard.

There was a terrible prolonged swelling roar, a brief flash of a strange golden fire from the entrance to the chapel and Richard stopped.

'Richard, if you love me!' I screamed.

He heard. When he looked toward me, there was horror and bewilderment in his face. The malicious smile had gone — the evil had left him. He was mine again.

'Richard, the axe!' bawled Ruane.

But it was Kresak who moved fast. He kicked out at the stumbling priest, and Ruane went down with a sickening crash. Richard saw what was happening and he saw Miaolo too. In the space of a few seconds he was putting together the events of the past weeks. I saw puzzlement, indecision, then understanding. He had incredibly fast reflexes, and the kind of mind that can instantly sum up a situation and react fast. It was like watching a healthy man come out of sleep — not a slow transition, but a swift change from unconsciousness to full alertness.

'Richard, get the axe — here!' I yelled, for Ruane was hurt.

Richard elbowed the screaming figure of Miaolo out of the way. He ran, very sure of himself, straight for the waiting Kresak. I didn't see what he did but Kresak was flung back in a heap just beside me. I got up then, but Richard had the axe in his hands. He looked at me, saw that I was all right and shook Ruane's shoulder.

'Ask him!' I yelled, pointing to Ruane.

'The head — strike off the head, then the Ulromes are free!' Ruane grated. Blood came from his mouth, 'Steel destroys the undead!'

Richard shuddered and sprang. I saw the axe head whirl in the mist with a dull flash of unpolished metal. There was a sickening brutal sound, then the blackened head flew, still gabbling, across the chapel floor, straight towards the dimly seen beast.

I heard a terrible wailing yell from the deadly thing; I saw the wide-open mouth, the lithe wet limbs, the flash of basilisk eyes; and that finished me. Unconsciousness — fainting — has been derided as a feminine wile; it wasn't then. I think it saved me from permanent mental damage. No one could have seen that last lunging leap and remain unharmed.

I saw the thing lunge for the blackened skull, and I saw enough.

Then shots rang out.

A grating transatlantic voice I knew, full of fury, called a warning.

'Still, or I fire!'

The cavern rang and rang again and boomed back primeval passions.

Death, rage, howls of furious deprivation and roars of righteous anger came back again and again from the bare faces of the rock. Eerie, ghastly sounds came from the monster from the sea. It was too much.

The last thing I remembered — and it would stay with me for all of my days, I knew that — was that deep and resounding last call from the depths of Ruane's huge chest:

'It is the Work of God!'

20

We were in a small, cluttered lounge
when I recovered consciousness; it was
obviously one of the old cottages near the
harbour, I heard the sound of the sea
though, and I shuddered.

'It's all over,' said Richard.

I got up and looked around.

Questions again. I wanted to ask
questions, but not yet.

I saw Ruane, limping. Charles Schofield
was there, and with him the big blond-
haired New York detective. I saw that he
wasn't really blond, more whitish hair, a
hard face and the concentrated gaze of
a man who was more than tough.

Joe Leckov was a truly hard man.
'Kresak's dead?' I asked.

I could not bring myself to ask about
the beast from the sea, not then, and, I
vowed to myself, not ever. The big man
nodded. 'Forget it all,' was all he said.

'Can't. You?'

I had addressed myself to the tall older man who had been the instrument of our salvation. I could go through it all mentally, and I could take reassurance in Richard Ulrome's grip on my shoulder, but I found myself shaking at the glimpses of the recent past. I felt bodily changes too.

My hormonal balance was way, way out of the norm.

'Oh, my god,' I said, turning to Richard and looking him straight in the brilliant ice-blue eyes. 'Richard, I'm pregnant.'

Why we come out with these things in the presence of what were after all complete strangers I do not know. The men, Schofield and Leckov tried to hold their expressions in that glacial all-knowing stare, but I could see that both were affected. Schofield allowed himself to raise his eyebrows slightly. Leckov managed a small downturn of the right side of his thin lips.

Richard grabbed me by both shoulders, and I was lost.

'You will forget all this, Anne,' he said. 'From now.'

'The thing — the beast — Richard, tell me!'

I was shouting, all composure lost, and only thoughts of a new life within me and Richard to hold on to, and Tony — dear, dear Tony, neglected for so long, to return to. My son. An heir for the Ulromes. And it could all have been so different, all could have been lost. I saw the heavy figure of a man of faith, and the dreadful sequence of events in the ruins came back with a devastating power.

'No!'

Ruane made the sign of the cross.

I took a minute or two, some of the heavy seconds in weeping, some trying to efface the memories of hate and the insensate.

★ ★ ★

'We're leaving now. Tonight,' Richard told me.

'Thank God.' I thought of Kresak. And Simon Miaolo. And then that last savage leap. Richard put a hand on my arm; I shivered and he saw my reaction. I couldn't bear him to touch me, and he knew it.

Someone passed Ruane a bottle. He looked at it, then he looked in my direction. I couldn't help him. I didn't have the words. It's like that sometimes: one has only so much strength. Ruane drank, and I said nothing.

I learned things later, as I have said.

The locals knew what we were about, not in detail but enough to work out why there was so much activity at the chapel. Memories are long on that coast. I think we owe them our lives, for there were enough of Kresak's kind at the Castle to have killed us to ensure our silence. But there were twenty or thirty of the sturdy locals, so Richard told me, all waiting on the cliff path, all with their fish-gutting knives. Richard told me about them when we were in the car. Ruane didn't accompany us. I didn't wish him to, however much I owed him. In those early days, I knew I could so easily have slid over the edge and let the torment claim me.

Not for a long time did I wish to be

reminded of what happened that night.

Certain things were unavoidable. There was the television news, for one thing, and the newspapers. The death of a man like Simon Miaolo would be reported widely. He had died in his bed at his North Yorkshire castle; that was the story.

They couldn't have handled it any other way.

Richard recovered with remarkable speed. A few days after our return to London, he told me he'd been thinking of trying to buy into a small boatyard on the southeast coast with what was left of the Ulrome money. There was enough, not a superfluity, but he'd be comfortable, provided he worked. He'd have to be at the yard for a few months, he said. He didn't mention marriage; he didn't try to touch me. Richard had the wit to realise that I had been through too much. In his own quiet way he was telling me he knew we might never again have the same kind of relationship; but that nevertheless he'd wait around. He came back to see me after a couple of weeks, when I'd got back into the routine of my old life. I still couldn't touch him, though we talked a good deal.

I asked questions about the things I'd hidden from.

By way of answer, he took from a briefcase the crucifix I had last seen hurtling toward the thing from the sea. I looked down and saw the marks on it.

'Ruane gave it to me,' he said. 'It stopped the beast.' Only the base of the cross bore the deep incisions; the pain-racked body was intact. The blind man's cross had saved us, for, just as Richard had been about to renew whatever pact was that the long-dead sixth Earl had made, the crucifix had crashed into its evil mouth. 'Ruane told me to keep the cross always,' said Richard. 'To remind me. To be sure of what happened — to be sure that it's over.'

I didn't want to hear any more, but I couldn't get rid of the worm of uncertainty that dug into me as the month went by. Richard told me about the boatyard; by then he was talking about our future, him, me and Tony. He didn't push me — and his quiet confidence gradually began to obliterate my unsaid fears. We wouldn't be rich, but we would be comfortable.

In the spring I spent the weekend at a small hotel near the yard. I didn't know that Richard had asked Charles Schofield and Freda Langdon down. I hadn't seen much of Freda lately, and I was glad to have her company. I'd spoken briefly before then to Charles Schofield but not about Monteine Castle. I had the impression that he was completely satisfied by what had transpired there. To this day, I don't know if Richard or Ruane or both told him what really happened; I knew I'd never ask him. I have never quite got over my mixed feeling about that urbane and disconcerting man.

His visit, however, prompted that last of the revelations about the frightful night in the chapel and perhaps also showed me the way to regain my happiness. Somehow the pleasant couple of days we had with Charles Schofield and Freda released the tensions in my mind — it wasn't anything in particular, nothing I could put my finger on, but when they left I was ready to ask Richard what had happened on Lammas Eve the previous year.

'You really want to know?'

'Yes.'

He nodded. 'I think you do, Anne.'

He was looking into a log fire, and the blue flames reminded me uncannily of the conflagration in the tomb. I shivered. 'But it is over, I promise, Anne. It can never touch the Ulromes again. They dynamited a thousand tons of rocks and earth onto the chapel — and there's no connection now between our family and that damned cliff. I'll tell you the rest because I think it's the only way of exorcising the thing from your mind.'

I knew it would be bad. But I needed to know the rest — we both knew it now.

'Please tell me.'

He didn't pretend he didn't want to tell me.

Ruane's intuition had been right. Briefly, Richard explained Mialo's plot and his own projected part in it. This much I knew. Richard had not been embittered by his experiences — the damage had been done to me. 'I think of it now as horrible and pathetic. Miaolo was a tired old man who had no more countries to buy, no more men to hurt, nothing to do but live on and on, trying to hold on to a life that had no more meaning but it's continuance.' I had never heard Richard so eloquent. I didn't pity Miaolo, but it was clear that something like compassion had moved Richard. He had thought deeply about the evil at Monteine. 'Even now I wonder if he lives on in some form we can't guess at.'

I sat upright then, terror sliding into my skull. It was going to be very bad.

Richard saw my white face and strained expression.

'Tell me,' I said, before he could retract.

'I will, but only because holding back now would harm us both. I have to tell you, Anne, it's as simple as that. You see, they were all half-blinded, so I don't suppose anyone else saw Miaolo at the end.'

The flare's brilliance had certainly blinded me.

'I saw what happened,' Richard said in a low intent voice. I wanted to comfort him. 'It reached to him, Anne, but the next morning there wasn't a mark on his body. I checked. There was an autopsy, and they couldn't have fiddled the report, no matter how much money they used. English pathologists aren't to be bought.'

I didn't know where it was leading.

'No,' I said. 'I suppose not.'

Without realising it, I had taken Richard's hand in mine; it felt right to hold him.

'But he was torn — I swear the sea-beast tore him. And the other thing, I saw that too.'

'What? What, Richard!'

'His face — his whole body. They changed. I swear there was a change. I saw it only for seconds, but Simon Mialo's body thickened, there was a line of dark fur on his neck, and his face was not that of a man.' Richard looked at me. I saw fear in his brilliant blue eyes. He was thinking of what might have happened to him. 'Miaolo had the mark of the beast.'

I gripped the scarred crucifix in my other hand.

'Oh Christ,' I said. 'Oh Christ.'

I asked him if we were really and truly to live without terror, and if Ruane could help us. Or if we could help Ruane.

'We're safe,' said Richard.

'We could give him — ' Then I stopped.

'Oblivion for a while,' said Richard. 'Would he thank us? He's suffered enough. Leave Ruane with his God.'

I thought of an unsigned Christmas card I'd received from New York. There was a message: 'It's over.'

I could never bear to watch the sea at night though, never.

THE END

Other titles in the
Linford Mystery Library:

F.B.I. SPECIAL AGENT

Gordon Landsborough

Cheyenne Charlie, Native American law student turned G-Man, is one of the Bureau's top agents. The New York office sends for him to investigate a sinister criminal gang called the Blond Boys. Their getaway cars somehow disappear in well-lit streets; they jam police radios; and now they've begun to add brutal murder to their daring robberies. Cheyenne follows a tangled trail that leads him to a desperate fight to the death in the beautiful scenery of the Catskill Mountains . . .